THE NEW YEAR'S QUILT

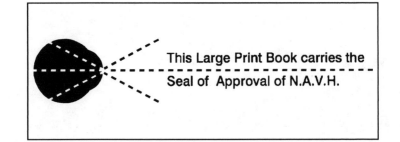

THE NEW YEAR'S QUILT

AN ELM CREEK QUILTS NOVEL

JENNIFER CHIAVERINI

THORNDIKE PRESS

An imprint of Thomson Gale, a part of The Thomson Corporation

THOMSON

™

GALE

Detroit • New York • San Francisco • New Haven, Conn. • Waterville, Maine • London

THOMSON
★ ™
GALE

Thorndike Press® Large Print Core.
The text of this Large Print edition is unabridged.
Other aspects of the book may vary from the original edition.
Set in 16 pt. Plantin.

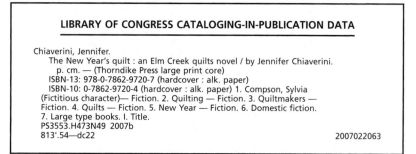

LIBRARY OF CONGRESS CATALOGING-IN-PUBLICATION DATA

Chiaverini, Jennifer.
  The New Year's quilt : an Elm Creek quilts novel / by Jennifer Chiaverini.
    p. cm. — (Thorndike Press large print core)
  ISBN-13: 978-0-7862-9720-7 (hardcover : alk. paper)
  ISBN-10: 0-7862-9720-4 (hardcover : alk. paper) 1. Compson, Sylvia
(Fictitious character)— Fiction. 2. Quilting — Fiction. 3. Quiltmakers —
Fiction. 4. Quilts — Fiction. 5. New Year — Fiction. 6. Domestic fiction.
7. Large type books. I. Title.
PS3553.H473N49 2007b
813'.54—dc22
                                         2007022063

Published in 2007 in arrangement with Simon & Schuster, Inc.

Printed in the United States of America on permanent paper
10 9 8 7 6 5 4 3 2 1

To Marlene and Leonard Chiaverini,
who know how to ring in
the New Year in style

ACKNOWLEDGMENTS

A bottle of fine champagne for Denise Roy, Maria Massie, Rebecca Davis, Annie Orr, Aileen Boyle, Honi Werner, Melanie Parks, David Rosenthal, and everyone at Simon & Schuster for supporting the Elm Creek Quilts series.

Party hats and noisemakers to Tara Shaughnessy, the world's most wonderful nanny, who plays with my boys and allows me time to write.

A chorus of "Auld Lang Syne" to the friends and family who have encouraged me through the years, especially Geraldine Neidenbach, Heather Neidenbach, Nic Neidenbach, Virginia Riechman, and Leonard and Marlene Chiaverini.

A sky full of fireworks for my husband, Marty, and my sons, Nicholas and Michael, for making every New Year the happiest yet.

CHAPTER ONE

Sylvia spun the radio dial through pop songs and talk shows until she came upon a station playing big band versions of holiday favorites. "We should break the news to her gently," Sylvia said. "We should sit her down, give her a stiff drink, and tell her in calm, soothing voices what we've done."

"You're likely to find that drink thrown in your face," Andrew retorted. "No, we should just tell her straight out, like tearing off a bandage. The sooner we tell her, the sooner she can start getting used to the idea."

Andrew knew his daughter better than Sylvia, but she doubted the direct approach would work. "How about this?" she suggested. "We'll say, 'Amy, dear, we have some bad news and some good news. The bad news is that we've gotten married. The good news is that since we got married on Christmas Eve, you won't have to buy us a separate wedding present.' "

"I don't like calling our marriage 'bad news.'"

"I don't either, but I'm sure that's how Amy will look at it."

"If she had any idea how happy I am that you finally consented to be my bride, I can't believe she'd refuse to be happy for us."

"Perhaps you should tell her how happy you are," said Sylvia. "Perhaps it will be as simple as that."

They considered that for a moment, and then in unison said, "I doubt it." Andrew chuckled, and Sylvia caressed his cheek before returning her gaze to the passing scenery, to snow-covered hills alight with the thin sunshine of a late December morning. She could not remember the last time she had been so content. Her husband of nearly two days was by her side, the pleasures of a winter honeymoon awaited them, and dear friends — a second family — would welcome them home to Elm Creek Manor after the New Year.

If only Andrew's daughter had not objected to the marriage, Sylvia's happiness would be complete.

She muffled a sigh, reluctant to allow Amy's perplexing disapproval to ruin her good spirits. If only she could rid her thoughts of Amy's last visit to Elm Creek

Manor, of her disappointed frown and the determined set to her shoulders when she reminded her father of Sylvia's stroke two years earlier, of how deeply Andrew had grieved when Amy's mother died of cancer. Sylvia and Andrew tried their best to put Amy's concerns to rest, but she had made up her mind, and nothing they said could persuade her that their marriage would not inevitably end in sorrow. "We all would love for you to have many, many years together," Amy had said, "but the end is going to be the same."

Eventually Andrew had heard enough. "If being by your mother's side throughout her illness taught me anything, it showed me that nothing matters but sharing your life with the people you love. Your mother had a great love of life. I'm ashamed that in her memory, you want me to curl up in a corner and wait to die."

Amy went scarlet as her father stormed off. Sylvia tried to reassure Amy that she had fully recovered from her stroke, she was in excellent health for her age, and she had sufficient resources to ensure that she would not become a burden to anyone, but Amy could not be appeased. Having failed to persuade her father, Amy appealed to Sylvia instead, but although Sylvia offered a sympathetic smile to soften her words, she resented the younger woman's ridiculous implications that she was on her deathbed and spoke more bluntly than she should have. "I'm sure you mean well," she said, "but we've made our decision, and I'm afraid you're just going to have to live with it."

Amy's startled expression told Sylvia that Amy had never expected her concerns to be dismissed so quickly. How could she have expected anything else? She should have known that Andrew had too much honor to withdraw a marriage proposal merely to please stubborn children, especially when it went against his own wishes and all common sense.

Sylvia sighed as the winter scenery rushed past her window, dreading their arrival in Hartford and the unpleasant scene that was sure to unfold when Andrew broke the news that they had married on Christmas Eve. She was grateful for the reprieve their two-day honeymoon in New York City would provide, but she knew they were only delaying the inevitable. In her more optimistic moments, Sylvia hoped that Amy would set aside her foolish objections when she realized the deed was done, her father was married, and nothing would change that.

More often, however, she feared that learning about the wedding after the fact would only inflame Amy's anger, and the recent months of estrangement between father and daughter would become a permanent condition.

The wedding had been lovely, for all that it had been pulled together in a matter of weeks. Sylvia and Andrew had hoped Amy would attend with her husband and three children, and naturally, they had invited Andrew's son, his wife, and their two daughters as well. Months earlier, Bob and Kathy had expressed misgivings when Andrew announced the engagement, but after the shock wore off, they seemed to accept his unexpected decision to remarry. Even Amy's husband had privately told the couple that he wished his own widowed father had been fortunate enough to find a second love as they had.

Sylvia and Andrew had invited everyone to Elm Creek Manor for Christmas without mentioning the wedding, a secret they had divulged only to the young couple that would act as witnesses and the judge who would officiate at the ceremony. They had intended to tell Andrew's children about the upcoming nuptials once they arrived at Elm Creek Manor, a few hours before Sylvia and Andrew would exchange their vows — enough time for them to get used to the idea but not enough for them to arrange flights home before the ceremony. Perhaps, Sylvia reluctantly admitted to herself, their plan had been misguided, even underhanded, and far more likely to backfire than to win the children over. Not that it mattered. Amy had turned down the invitation with a weak excuse about wanting to spend a quiet Christmas at home, and Bob, unwilling to risk angering his sister by appearing to take sides, had stayed away, too.

They had missed a beautiful wedding. Sarah McClure, Sylvia's quilting apprentice and business partner, and her husband, Matt, had staged a holiday wonderland. The candlelit ballroom of Elm Creek Manor glimmered with poinsettias, ribbon, and evergreen boughs. Andrew had built a fire in the large fireplace, then added the nostalgic decoration of the nativity scene Sylvia's father had brought back from a visit to the Bergstroms' ancestral home in Baden-Baden, Germany. The youngest Elm Creek Quilter, Summer Sullivan, had taken charge of the musical entertainment, setting Christmas carols wafting on air fragrant with the scents of pine and cinnamon and roasted apples. Just across the dance floor, the cook and two assistants — his daughter and her best friend, or so Sylvia had overheard — placed silver trays of hors d'oeuvres and cookies on a long table and prepared the buffet for hot dishes still simmering in the kitchen. Someone had opened the curtains covering the floor to ceiling windows on the south wall, and snowflakes fell gently against the windowpanes.

Sylvia could not have imagined a more festive place to spend a Christmas Eve.

Soon guests began to fill the ballroom — the Elm Creek Quilters and their families, other friends from the nearby town of Waterford, college students Sylvia had befriended while participating in various research projects, and Katherine Quigley, the mayor, who was one of the few people in on Sylvia and Andrew's secret. Cocktails were served, followed by a delicious meal of roasted Cornish game hen with cranberry walnut dressing that reminded Sylvia all over again why some quilters claimed they came to Elm Creek Quilt Camp for the food alone. Summer put some big band tunes on the CD player and led her boyfriend to the dance floor. Other couples joined them, and soon the room was alive with laughter, music, and the warmth of friendship.

"I don't think I've ever had a happier

Christmas Eve," said Sylvia as she danced with Andrew. "I hate to see it end."

"Is that so?" He regarded her, eyebrows raised. "Does that mean you've changed your mind?"

"Of course not," she said, lowering her voice as the song ended. "In fact, I was just about to suggest we get started."

He brought her hands to his lips. "I was hoping you'd say that."

Sylvia signaled to Sarah, who found Mayor Quigley in the crowd and told her that the time had come. Andrew smiled as Sylvia fidgeted with her bouquet. "Nervous?"

"Not at all," she said. "I just hope our friends will forgive us."

"They'll have to, once we remind them that you and I never said anything about waiting until June."

"May I have everyone's attention, please?" called Sarah over the noise of the crowd. Someone turned down the volume on the stereo. "On behalf of Sylvia and Andrew and everyone who considers Elm Creek Manor a home away from home, thank you for joining us on this very special Christmas Eve."

Everyone applauded, except Andrew, who straightened his tie, and Sylvia, who took the arm of her groom.

"It is also my honor and great pleasure,"

said Sarah, "to inform you that you are here not only to celebrate Christmas, but also the wedding of our two dear friends, Sylvia Compson and Andrew Cooper."

Gasps of surprise and excitement quickly gave way to cheers. Sylvia felt her cheeks growing hot as their many friends turned to them, applauding and calling their names.

"You said June," one of the Elm Creek Quilters protested.

"No, *you* said June," retorted Sylvia.

"But I already bought my dress and picked out your gown!"

All present burst into laughter, and, joining in as loudly as anyone, Sarah held up her hands for quiet. "If you would all gather around, Andrew would like to escort his beautiful bride down the aisle."

The crowd parted to make way for the couple, and Summer slipped away to the CD player. As the first strains of Bach's "Jesu, Joy of Man's Desiring" filled the air, Sylvia and Andrew walked among their guests to where the mayor waited.

To Sylvia, every moment of the simple ceremony rang as true as a crystal chime. They pledged to be true, faithful, respectful, and loving to each other until the end of their days. They listened, hand in hand, as the mayor reminded them of the significance and irrevocability of their promises. They exchanged rings, and when they kissed, the room erupted in cheers and applause. As Sarah and Matt came forward to sign the marriage license, Sylvia looked out upon the assembled friends wiping their eyes and smiling, and she knew that she and Andrew had wed surrounded by love, exactly as they knew they should.

If only Andrew's children and grandchildren had come to share this moment. If only they could be as happy for Sylvia and Andrew as their friends were. Sylvia looked up at her new husband and saw in his eyes that he shared her wistful thoughts.

She reached up to touch his cheek. He put his hand over hers, and smiled.

It had truly been a marvelous wedding, exactly the celebration she and Andrew had wanted. Even the Elm Creek Quilters had enjoyed themselves too much to complain that they would have to abandon their own plans for a June wedding.

The only shadow cast upon their happiness was the absence of Andrew's family.

Sylvia, who considered herself something of an expert on the subject of familial estrangement and its consequences, knew that Amy was the key. If they could win her

18

over, the others would follow, relieved to see family harmony restored. Amy had clearly inherited her father's stubbornness, but with any luck, she had also inherited his kind heart.

As Bing Crosby crooned "I'll Be Home for Christmas," Sylvia forced her worries aside and reached into the back seat for her tote bag. Mindful of Andrew's travel mug in the cup holder between them, still half-full of coffee from the Bear's Paw Inn, she took out her current work-in-progress, a patchwork quilt in blues, golds, and whites with touches of black scattered here and there wherever the whim had struck her. The quilt had a wintry feel to it, or so she had always thought, and it had suited her to work on it when the days were short and the nights long and cold. In recent months, she had decided to finish the quilt once and for all, and not only for the satisfaction of crossing another item off her Unfinished Fabric Object list. The one task that remained was to sew on the binding, the outermost strip of fabric that concealed the raw edges of the quilt top, batting, and lining. Usually Sylvia found such simple handwork tedious, the least creative and enjoyable task of the quilting art, but today she welcomed the distraction.

Andrew glanced over as she threaded her needle. "Is that our wedding quilt?"

"I'm sorry, dear, but it isn't." Deftly Sylvia drew her needle through the raw edge of the quilt, hid the knot within the batting, and began sewing the binding to the back of the quilt with small, barely visible ladder stitches. "It's only a lap quilt, not big enough for our bed. You'll have to wait a few months if you want a wedding quilt from me."

"Maybe the Elm Creek Quilters will make us one."

They were her dearest, closest friends, so perhaps they would. On the other hand . . . "After they've had a chance to recover from their surprise, they might."

Andrew grinned. "And if they forgive us for denying them the wedding of their dreams?"

"Precisely." In sharp contrast to Andrew's children, the Elm Creek Quilters had been so delighted by the announcement of their engagement that they had been carried away with wedding-planning enthusiasm. Sylvia felt a twinge of guilt for spoiling their plans after her friends had gone to the trouble of choosing the wedding cake, finding the perfect wedding gown in a bridal magazine, and setting the date for the ceremony after

20

a comparison of their schedules ruled out half the Saturdays in June, but it had to be done. Sylvia and Andrew couldn't bear the thought of putting on an enormous production knowing that his children would refuse to attend. This way, they could make themselves believe that Amy and Bob and their families would have come for Christmas if they had known that a wedding would take place. This way, in the years to come, Andrew's children would not be haunted by guilt for refusing to attend their father's wedding.

Sylvia hoped to spare Amy and Bob regrets they were too young to know lay ahead of them.

"Though it's not our wedding quilt," Andrew said, "it still must be important or you wouldn't have brought it along on our honeymoon."

"It is, indeed." Sylvia spread it open on her lap so he could glimpse more of the colorful patchwork, although he would not truly be able to appreciate the quilt's loveliness in such cramped quarters. "It's a quilt for the season. I call it New Year's Reflections."

"Reflections, not resolutions?"

"Reflections should precede resolutions, or so I've always thought."

Andrew shook his head. "I don't believe in making New Year's resolutions. If someone needs to change, they should change, and not wait for the New Year to do it."

"Some people don't have your self-discipline," said Sylvia, smiling. "Some people need an important occasion to herald a time for change."

"Some people, meaning yourself?"

"Perhaps. I'm very much in favor of New Year's resolutions, and I support anyone who chooses to make one. They are a sign of optimism and hope in an increasingly cynical world. Someone who makes a New Year's resolution is declaring that they have hope, that they believe they can improve their lives, that we can change our world for the better."

"You don't need to change. I wouldn't change a thing about you."

"Spoken like a true newlywed," teased Sylvia. "It's very good that you don't want to change me, because you can't, you know. And it's not because women of a certain age are set in their ways or any such nonsense. No one can make another person change. One has to change oneself."

But that did not mean a caring friend couldn't point out a new direction to someone headed down the wrong road, and hope they took heed. The New Year's Reflections quilt never failed to remind her of that, or that a new path chosen without careful reflection would lead even the most resolute traveler in a broad circle, back to where she had begun, and no better off than when she had set out on her journey.

Andrew fell silent while Sylvia methodically sewed down the binding, each stitch bringing her closer to the completion of an on-again, off-again quilt nearly six years in the making. Out of the corner of one eye, she observed Andrew frowning slightly as he pondered the mystery of her quilt's presence on their honeymoon. "Did you bring the quilt because last year you resolved to finish it before midnight on New Year's Eve, and you're running out of time?"

"No," said Sylvia with a little laugh. "I brought it along because it's a gift for Amy."

"But we sent the kids their Christmas presents weeks ago."

"It's not a Christmas gift. It's a New Year's gift." Sylvia hesitated before deciding to tell him the whole truth. He was, after all, her husband now. "It's a gift to thank her for accepting my marriage to her father."

Andrew shot her a look of utter bewilderment. "But she didn't," he said, quickly returning his gaze to the road ahead. "She doesn't. She made that perfectly clear when I told her I was going to marry you whether she liked it or not. Sylvia, I think you should prepare yourself. This peace offering of yours — it's a pretty quilt and a nice gesture, but it might not be enough. This whole trip might be a waste of time."

"I refuse to believe that," said Sylvia. This attempt at reconciliation was for the newlyweds as much as it was for Amy. It would do them some small good to know they had tried, even if Amy rebuffed them.

And while it was true that Amy had not accepted her father's engagement and almost certainly would not welcome news of his marriage, perhaps by the time the New Year dawned, she would have a change of heart. Sylvia would put her trust in the power of the season to inspire new beginnings, even if Andrew did not.

As they drove through eastern Pennsylvania on their way to New York, Sylvia chatted with Andrew and worked on the New Year's Reflections quilt, every stitch a silent prayer that Andrew and his daughter would reconcile. She could not bear to be the cause of their estrangement. She knew all too well the ache of loneliness that filled a heart that learned forgiveness too late.

For more than fifty years, bitterness and grief had separated Sylvia from the home she loved — and the sister whom she blamed unfairly as the cause of all her sorrow. Every New Year had offered her an opportunity to start over, but she had stubbornly awaited an apology that never came, an apology she perhaps did not deserve. Only after Claudia's death did Sylvia return to Elm Creek Manor and discover that her sister had missed her and had longed for her return. If only Sylvia had not cut off her ties so completely, Claudia might have been able to find her, to send word to her, to offer the apology Sylvia had resolutely awaited. If only Sylvia had not allowed obstinate pride to prevent her from reaching out to Claudia first.

Sylvia would not allow Andrew and Amy to repeat her mistakes. Some good had to come of her hard-earned lessons. Their disagreement was not longstanding; surely the wound would heal if they tended it quickly and did not allow the infection of anger to take deeper root.

Sylvia tucked the needle into the edge of the binding and held up the quilt to inspect her work. The double-fold bias strip of dark blue cotton lay smooth and straight, without a single pucker, a perfect frame for the

25

twelve blue-and-gold patchwork blocks of her own invention, twelve variations of the traditional Mother's Favorite block.

Claudia probably would have had something to say about Sylvia's choice. Each daughter had longed to be their mother's favorite, and as a child, Sylvia had wavered between fear and certainty that she wasn't it. Claudia probably would not have believed that Sylvia had chosen the pattern despite its name, not because of it. It was visually striking, with a four-inch central square set on point by white triangles and framed by narrow strips of blue. Triangles pieced from lighter blue trapezoids and white triangles made up the corners of the block, creating a distant resemblance to the better-known Pineapple block. But Sylvia had complicated an already difficult pattern by substituting miniature patchwork blocks for the solid, four-inch squares in the centers. These blocks she had indeed chosen for their names, for their symbolism, for the memories of long-ago New Year's celebrations that came to mind whenever she worked upon the quilt.

Sylvia ran a hand over the patchwork surface, wishing the pieces of her life fit together with such precision. It was difficult to look to the year ahead with anticipation and hope when she could not help glancing over her shoulder with regret at the mistakes of the past. Throughout her long, lonely exile from Elm Creek Manor, picking out the threads of her past mistakes had become a New Year's Eve tradition for her, as much a part of the holiday as the countdown to midnight and "Auld Lang Syne."

It had not always been that way. She had not learned that melancholy habit at her mother's knee, or from any of the other Bergstrom women who passed down family traditions through the generations. When Sylvia was a girl, the Bergstrom family ushered in the New Year with joy and merriment whether the world beyond the gray stone walls of the family home was at peace or at war, enjoying prosperity or enduring hardship.

A lifetime ago, as 1925 approached, the Bergstrom family had had much to be thankful for: the comfortable manor large enough to accommodate their extended family, the sustenance their farm provided, the company of those they loved, and unprecedented success and prosperity mirroring the nation's rise in fortune. During the few years before, newly wealthy businessmen from as far away as Chicago and New York City had flocked to Elm Creek

Manor, eager to add prized Bergstrom Thoroughbreds to their growing lists of possessions. Even little Sylvia understood that they wanted to impress friends and rivals and to prove themselves the equals of the "old money" families who had kept Bergstrom Thoroughbreds in their stables almost from the time Sylvia's great-grandfather had founded the business before the Civil War. Although Sylvia mourned the departure of each elegant mare or proud stallion, she did not complain. She knew the family owed their livelihood to these stout businessmen in fine suits who spoke in brash accents as they puffed their cigars and watched her father and uncles put the horses through their paces. She was old enough to understand that each horse the men bought meant food on their table, new dresses and shoes to wear to school, and money to pay her mother's doctor bills.

Sylvia's favorite cousin, Elizabeth, had more reason than any Bergstrom for happiness that season, as she had recently become engaged to her longtime sweetheart, Henry Nelson, a young man from a neighboring farm. The wedding plans had already begun in earnest despite the holiday because, much to Sylvia's dismay, Henry and Elizabeth planned to marry at the end of March and move to California, where Henry had purchased a cattle ranch.

Sylvia had never liked Henry. Whenever he came around, Elizabeth forgot her favorite little cousin and went off riding or walking or picking apples with Henry instead. When he stayed for supper, he took Sylvia's chair at the table without even asking permission, as if he had more right to sit at Elizabeth's side than Sylvia. No matter how often Sylvia scowled at him or spoke impertinently or squeezed herself between Henry and Elizabeth when they sat by the fire turning pages of a book, Henry seemed stupidly unaware of how unwelcome he was. Whenever Elizabeth visited from Harrisburg, Henry included himself in every holiday gathering at Elm Creek Manor, and he wasn't even family.

But he would be, soon. Sylvia felt sick at heart as she realized that when Henry and Elizabeth married, she would lose her favorite playmate and confidante forever.

Even Elizabeth's promise that Sylvia and Claudia could be flower girls at the wedding did nothing to console her. Instead, Sylvia strengthened her resolve to persuade Henry to go away and never come back. If he went to California without Elizabeth, that would be best of all, but Sylvia would be satisfied if he stayed on the other side of the fence separating the Nelson farm from the Bergstroms'.

Sylvia tried her best, but she was not naturally devious and she had to be careful not to raise the ire of her parents, aunts, and uncles, who did not seem to realize that Henry had to be stopped. One day, inspiration struck as she came upon Henry waiting in the parlor while Elizabeth finished a wedding gown fitting upstairs with Sylvia's mother and aunts. "Is Elizabeth still crying?" she asked him, strolling into the room and plopping down on her grandma's favorite upholstered chair.

Henry regarded her warily. "What do you mean?"

Sylvia fingered a loose thread on the ottoman and did her best to look nonchalant. "Oh, you know. She's always crying these days. Grandpa says she's 'turning on the waterworks.' "

"Is that so?" Henry's brow furrowed. "Do you know what she's crying about?"

"I'm not sure. She never cries when she's with me." Sylvia felt a thrill of delight when Henry's frown deepened. "But I heard her tell my mama . . ."

"What?" Henry prompted.

"I'm not supposed to listen at doors."

"I won't tell anyone."

"Promise?"

Henry nodded, barely containing his impatience. "Of course. Go on. What did Elizabeth say?"

"She told my mama that it would break her heart to go to California and never see her family again."

Henry sat back in his chair. "She said that?"

Sylvia nodded. What Elizabeth had really said was that she would miss Elm Creek Manor terribly and she dreaded the moment of her departure, but she loved Henry and it would break her heart to stay behind and let him go to California without her. That was what Elizabeth had said, but Sylvia knew Elizabeth and she understood the real meaning hidden behind her words. Henry was wrong to take her away, and since Elizabeth was too afraid to hurt his feelings, it was up to Sylvia to tell him the truth.

Henry rose and strode from the room. Sylvia jumped up and peered through the doorway after him, but her heart sank in dismay when she spied him crossing the black marble floor of the front foyer on his way to the grand oak staircase instead of slinking off down the west wing hallway to the back door. Jolted by guilty alarm, she hurried off the way Henry should have chosen, barely pausing to pull on her boots and coat before racing outside into the snow.

She hid out in the barn, keeping warm in the hayloft while the cows scuffed their hooves and lowed complaints below. She had missed lunch, and her stomach growled. When her mittened fingers grew numb, she had no choice but to return indoors. Henry's boots no longer stood in a puddle of melted snow just inside the back door. She tried to find encouragement in his absence, but her stomach was a knot of worry.

She tiptoed upstairs to the nursery to find her mother and Claudia sitting on the window seat reading a book. Claudia glared, accusatory and triumphant. Sylvia could not bear to meet her mother's gaze.

"Claudia, darling, would you please wait for me downstairs?" Sylvia's mother asked.

"Now you're going to get it," Claudia whispered, brushing past Sylvia on the way out the door.

"Sylvia, come here." Her mother patted the window seat.

Sylvia obeyed, dragging her feet across the nursery floor. She sat beside her mother, eyes downcast, and did not resist when her mother took her hands. "Goodness, Sylvia," she exclaimed, chafing her daughter's hands with her own. "You're half frozen. Where have you been hiding?"

"In the barn."

"I would have guessed the stable — you love the horses so much."

The stable would have been Sylvia's first choice, but she would have risked discovery there. Her father and uncles were in and out of the stable all day, tending the horses.

Mama was silent for a moment, but then she sighed. "Darling, I know how much you love Elizabeth. I know you're going to miss her when she goes to California. But Elizabeth loves Henry, and she is going to marry him. Being mean to him won't change that."

Tears sprang into Sylvia's eyes. Henry had told on her. She had always known he couldn't be trusted.

"I suppose I've been too lenient. I've excused your little pranks because of the holidays, because I know how much you admire your cousin, how important it is for you to be her favorite . . ." The distant look in her mother's eyes suddenly disappeared, and she fixed Sylvia with a firm but loving gaze. "I'm sure you want what's best for Elizabeth. She loves Henry, and Henry loves her. Our family has known him since long before you were born. If I thought he wouldn't make her happy, if I suspected for one moment that he wasn't a good man, don't you think I'd be with her right this moment trying to talk her out of it?"

"I . . ." Sylvia had not thought about it. "I guess so."

"Once, long ago, I almost married the wrong man for the wrong reasons, so trust me when I say I've learned to recognize a bad match —" Mama caught herself. "But that's a story for another day. The problem, Sylvia, isn't Elizabeth's choice or your feelings about it. The real problem is that you lied."

Surprised, Sylvia blurted, "No, I didn't."

"Yes, you did. It was very naughty of you to tell Henry that Elizabeth doesn't want to go to California with him. It was wrong for you to make him think he was making her unhappy."

But he *was* making her unhappy. He made Elizabeth cry. Elizabeth didn't want to leave Elm Creek Manor; Sylvia had heard her tell Mama so. "But I didn't lie. What I said was true, I know it was."

"Sylvia." The single word, gently spoken, was reproach enough for Sylvia. She knew she hadn't lied, but Mama believed she had and could not hide her disappointment. Sylvia wished she had never come in from the barn. The one rule her father and the other grown-ups of the household upheld before all others was that no one should upset Mama. She had suffered a terrible illness that had injured her heart when she was a little girl no bigger than Sylvia. Although Father could not stop Mama from romping with the children in the nursery or riding her favorite horse, his worried admonitions alarmed the girls and made them cautious. Whenever Mama was forced to take to her bed, Sylvia hid from Dr. Granger as he raced up the steps, black bag in hand, certain he would scold her for whatever she had done to make his visit necessary.

What if, by trying to keep Elizabeth close, Sylvia had harmed Mama?

Sylvia flung her arms around her mother. "I'm sorry," she said, her voice muffled by her mother's sweater.

Mama stroked Sylvia's long, tangled curls. "It's all right, darling. I know you won't do it again. I can't ask you to like Henry, but for all our sakes, please try to be kinder to him. Perhaps for the New Year you can make a fresh start. Elizabeth loves him. Perhaps you can resolve to try to love him a little, too."

Sylvia couldn't imagine ever feeling anything but anger and resentment for Henry, especially now that he had turned out to be a big tattletale, but she nodded to please her mother. She wished the grown-ups understood that she was only doing what was best for everyone. She could not imagine how Elizabeth would ever be happy, so far away in California with only dreary Henry for company.

Concealing her dislike wouldn't be easy, but Sylvia would have to try because the alternative was to hide in her room until the holidays passed, and she couldn't bear to miss out on all the fun. This year, Great-Aunt Lucinda had decided to revive an old tradition her parents and aunt had brought to America from Germany, a Sylvester Ball on New Year's Eve. The last time the Bergstrom family had celebrated the night of Holy St. Sylvester was before Sylvia was born, so Sylvia had no memory of those happy occasions. Great-Aunt Lucinda said there would be dancing, singing, and lots of delicious treats to eat and drink. She also promised Sylvia that she and Claudia could stay up until midnight to welcome the New Year. Sylvia knew that any more naughtiness could cost her that privilege, so she vowed to behave herself, at least until January 2.

Snow fell on the morning of December 31. Sylvia and Claudia spent most of the day outside, sledding and building snowmen, until their mother called them inside for a nap. Claudia went inside without complaint, but Sylvia balked at going to bed in the middle of the day. Only when her mother warned her that she would never be able to stay up until midnight if she did not rest first did she reluctantly come inside.

Cousin Elizabeth passed her on the landing, breathless, her golden curls bouncing, her eyes alight with pleasure and mischief. How could Sylvia not adore her? "Hello, little Sylvia," Elizabeth sang, sweeping her up in a hug. "Where are you off to on this last day of the year?"

When Sylvia reported that she had been sent to bed, Elizabeth gave her a quizzical frown. "You don't look sleepy to me."

"I'm not," said Sylvia, glum. "Naps are for babies."

"I couldn't agree more. Come on." Elizabeth took her by the hand and quickly led her up another flight of stairs to the nursery. "This is your first big dance, and we don't have a lot of time to get ready."

Sylvia threw a quick, anxious glance over her shoulder, but no one was around to report to her mother. "Claudia will tell on me when I don't come to bed."

"Oh, don't worry about her. When I passed your room she was already snoring away. She'll never know what time you came in."

Sylvia hated to disobey her mother so soon after resolving to be good, but a chance to spend time alone with Elizabeth might not come again for a very long while, if ever. She tightened her grasp on her cousin's hand until they shut the nursery door behind them. Elizabeth slid a chair in place beneath the doorknob. "That'll give you time to hide should anyone come snooping," said Elizabeth. "We'll have to keep our voices down. Take off your shoes and show me what you know."

Sylvia took off her Mary Janes and bravely demonstrated the few ballet steps her mother had taught her and Claudia, half-afraid that Elizabeth would laugh and send her off to take a nap after all. Then she stood in first position, awaiting her cousin's verdict. "Well, you're not a lost cause," said Elizabeth. "In fact, that's a very good beginning. I started out in ballet myself. Your aunt Millie insisted. But that's not the kind of dancing we're going to be doing tonight. You have a lot to learn and not a lot of time."

Elizabeth took her hands and, over the next two hours, introduced Sylvia to grown-up dances she called the fox-trot, the quickstep, and one Sylvia had seen her parents do — the waltz. When Sylvia proved to be an apt pupil, Elizabeth praised her and taught her the tango and the Charleston. Dancing hand in hand with her cousin, gliding over the wood floor in her stocking feet, smothering laughter and asking questions in stage whispers, Sylvia realized she had not been so happy since before Elizabeth announced her engagement. Henry Nelson seemed very far away, as if he had already gone off to California, alone.

Sylvia gladly would have danced on until the guests arrived, but suddenly Elizabeth glanced at the clock and exclaimed that they had better return downstairs quickly and get dressed if they didn't want the neighbors to catch them in their underthings. Giggling, Sylvia crept downstairs to her bedroom, where she rumpled her quilt, opened the blinds, and woke Claudia, who never suspected her sister had not just risen from a nap herself.

Soon Mama bustled in, slim and elegant in her black velveteen gown, to make sure the girls had scrubbed their hands and faces and put on their best winter dresses. Sylvia's was only a hand-me-down, Claudia reminded her, while her own was new; Grandma had sewn it for her especially.

"Now, girls, don't bicker," said Mama, brushing the tangles from Sylvia's hair and tying it back with a ribbon that matched the dark green trim of Claudia's outgrown dress. Sylvia wanted to protest that she wasn't bickering, that Claudia was the only one who had spoken, but she had already upset Mama once that day and didn't want to push her luck, even if it meant letting Claudia get the last word.

Soon the guests arrived, friends and neighbors from nearby farms and the town of Waterford, two miles away. Sylvia stuck close to Elizabeth until Henry Nelson arrived with his family and Elizabeth dashed off to welcome them. Sylvia scowled at them from across the foyer as Elizabeth kissed his cheek and helped his mother out of her coat. It didn't matter. When the dance began, Elizabeth would come back. Hadn't she said that Sylvia was a swell partner? Hadn't they spent two hours practicing? Hadn't she declared that together they would show everyone what Bergstrom girls could do?

The Sylvester Ball began with a supper of lentil soup, followed by pork and sauerkraut.

Pork roasted with apples was one of Sylvia's favorite dishes, and she loved Great-Aunt Lucinda's sauerkraut, chopped much finer than Great-Aunt Lydia's, mildly flavored, and thickened with barley. Since the Bergstroms enjoyed pork and sauerkraut every New Year — although they usually ate the meal on New Year's Day rather than the night before — Sylvia was surprised to see some of their neighbors wrinkling their noses at the aromatic, fermented cabbage. "Try it," she urged Rosemary, Henry's younger sister, but Rosemary shook her head and gingerly pushed the shredded cabbage around her plate with her fork. A few of the more reluctant guests took tentative bites only after Great-Aunt Lucinda insisted that the meal would bring them good luck in the year to come. Germans considered pigs to be good luck, she explained, because back in the old days, a farm family who had a pig to feed them through the long, cold winter was fortunate indeed. "Why do you think children save their pennies in piggy banks," she asked, "when any animal could have done as well?" And since cabbage leaves were symbolic of money, a meal of pork and sauerkraut would help secure good fortune throughout the New Year.

"Dig in, son," Uncle George advised his

41

future son-in-law, and Henry gamely took an impressive portion of sauerkraut. Sylvia wished he had refused. That would have convinced everyone that he didn't belong in the family.

Afterward, the party resumed in the ballroom, where the musicians Uncle George had hired from Harrisburg struck up a lively tune that beckoned couples to the dance floor. Sylvia looked around for Elizabeth, but Claudia grabbed Sylvia's hand and dragged her over to a corner where they could play ring-around-the-rosie in time to the music. Sylvia had no interest whatsoever in playing a baby game to what was obviously a quickstep, but when she saw Elizabeth on Henry's arm, she gloomily played along to appease Claudia. When the song ended, she slipped away and wove through the crowd to Elizabeth, but now her beautiful cousin was waltzing with Uncle George, and Sylvia knew she would be scolded if she interrupted.

Her turn would come, she told herself, but dance after dance went by, and always Elizabeth was with Henry, or her father, or Henry's father, or one of her uncles. Mostly she was with Henry. When she finally sat out a dance, Sylvia raced to her side. "There you are," Elizabeth exclaimed, and as far as

Sylvia could tell, her cousin was delighted to see her. "Are you having a good time?"

Sylvia was miserable, but Elizabeth could easily fix that. "Can I have a turn to dance with you?"

Elizabeth fanned herself with her hand. "Absolutely, right after I rest with some of your father's punch." She looked around for Henry, but Sylvia quickly volunteered to get Elizabeth a cup, and she hurried off through the crowd of dancers and onlookers to the fireplace at the opposite end of the room.

Her father sat by the fireside, joking with his brothers and Henry's father, who waited impatiently to sample her father's renowned *Feuerzangenbowle*. Into a large black kettle he had emptied two bottles of red wine, some of the last of his wine cellar. Sylvia caught the aroma of rich wine and spices — cinnamon, allspice, cardamom — and the sweet fruity fragrances of lemon and orange. Her father stirred the steaming brew, careful to keep the fire just high enough to heat the punch without boiling.

"At this rate it'll be midnight before we can wet our whistles, Fred," one of the neighbors teased.

"If you're too thirsty to wait, have some coffee and save the punch for more patient men," Sylvia's father retorted with a grin. "Sylvia can show you to the kitchen."

Sylvia froze while the men laughed, relaxing only when she realized none of the men intended to take her father up on his offer. Although many of their neighbors of German descent had brewed their own beer long before Prohibition, few could obtain fine European wines like those Father's customers offered him to sweeten their deals. They wouldn't leave the fireside without a glass of Father's famous punch, and neither would Sylvia. She was determined to serve Elizabeth before Henry did, to prove just how unnecessary he was.

Father traded the long-handled spoon for a sturdy pair of tongs, grasped a sugar cone, and held it over the kettle. With his left hand, he slowly poured rum over the sugar cone, or *Zuckerhut* as the older Bergstroms called it, and let the liquor soak in to the fine, compressed sugar. At Father's signal, Uncle William came forward, withdrew a wooden skewer from the fire, and set the sugar cone on fire. Sylvia watched, entranced, as the bluish flame danced across the sugar cone and carmelized the sugar, which dripped into the steaming punch below. When the flame threatened to flicker out, her father poured more rum over the

Zuckerhut until the bottle was empty and the sugar melted away. With a sigh of anticipated pleasure, the uncles and neighbors pressed forward with their cups as Father picked up the ladle and began to serve. Sylvia found herself pushed to the back of the crowd, and not until the last of the eager grown-ups had taken their mugs from the fireside was she able to approach her father.

He eyed her with amusement. "This isn't a drink for little girls."

"It's not for me." Sylvia glanced over her shoulder and spied Elizabeth still seated where Sylvia had left her, laughing with Rosemary, Henry's sister. "It's for Elizabeth."

"I don't know if Elizabeth should be drinking this, either."

"If she's not old enough for punch, maybe she's not old enough to get married."

Her father was so astonished that he rocked back on his heels and laughed. Sylvia flushed and turned away, but her father caught her by the arm. "Very well, little miss, you may take your cousin some punch. Mind you don't sample it along the way."

Sylvia nodded and held very still as her father ladled steaming punch into her teacup. With small, careful steps, she skirted the dance floor and made her way back to Elizabeth. She scowled to find that Henry had replaced Rosemary at Elizabeth's side.

"Here you go," Sylvia said, presenting the cup to her cousin. Elizabeth thanked her and took it with both hands. Pleased with herself and relieved that she had accomplished the task without spilling a single drop, she sat down on the floor at her cousin's feet, ready to block her path should Henry take her hand and attempt to lead her to the dance floor.

"Your father won't be happy to see you drinking," Henry warned in a low voice that Sylvia barely overheard.

"My father is the last person who should complain about anyone's drinking."

"He's not drinking tonight."

"Yes, and don't you find it interesting that he can exercise some self-control while all the family is watching, and yet he can't muster up any fortitude at home?"

Sylvia heard Henry shift in his chair to take Elizabeth's cup. "Maybe you've had too much already. You're not used to this stuff."

"Henry, that's truly not necessary. I only had a sip —"

Infuriated, Sylvia spun around to glare at him. "My daddy made that punch and it's very good. You're just mad because I brought it to her instead of you. You have to spoil everything!"

Henry regarded her for a moment, expressionless, his hands frozen around Elizabeth's as she clutched the cup. A thin wisp of steam rose between them. "Never mind," said Henry, dropping his hands to his lap. "If you want to drink it, drink it."

"No, no, that's fine." Elizabeth passed him the cup so quickly he almost spilled it. "I'm not thirsty after all."

Henry clearly didn't believe her, but he set the cup aside. "Do you want to go for a walk?"

"I promised Sylvia I would dance with her."

Sylvia was too overcome with relief that Elizabeth had not forgotten her promise to pay any attention to Henry's reply. When he rose and walked away, she promptly scooted his chair closer to Elizabeth's and sat down upon it. Absently, Elizabeth took her hand and watched the dancers in silence. Sylvia pretended not to notice that her cousin was troubled. Elizabeth was here, she was going to give Sylvia her turn, and Sylvia was not going to probe her with questions that might make her too unhappy or distracted to dance.

At last the song ended, and after a momentary pause another lively tune began. Elizabeth smiled at her and said, "Are you ready to cut a rug?"

Sylvia nodded and took her hand. Elizabeth led her to the dance floor and counted out the first few beats, then threw herself into a jaunty Charleston. Sylvia struggled to keep up at first, distracted by the music that drowned out Elizabeth's counting and the many eyes upon them, but she stoked her courage and persevered. She felt a thrill of delight when she spotted Claudia watching them, mouth open in astonishment. Henry's disgruntled frown filled her with satisfaction, and she kicked higher and smiled broader just to spite him. Most of the guests had put aside their own dancing to gather in a circle around the two cousins as they danced side by side. Sylvia mirrored her graceful cousin's spirited steps as closely as she could, praying her family and the guests wouldn't notice her mistakes.

All too soon the song ended. Breathless and laughing, Elizabeth took Sylvia's hand and led her in a playful, sweeping bow. She blew kisses to the crowd as she guided Sylvia from the dance floor while the musicians struck up a slow foxtrot and the couples resumed dancing. To Sylvia's chagrin, Elizabeth made her way directly to the far side of the room, where Henry waited beside one of the tall windows overlooking the elm grove and the creek, invisible in the darkness. He had eyes only for Elizabeth as they approached.

"You've been practicing," he remarked, smiling at her with fond amusement.

"I have to do something to keep myself busy when I'm bored and lonely back home in Harrisburg and you're tending the farm up here. Did you think I sat home every night pining for you?"

"I had hoped so." He slid his arm around Elizabeth's waist and pulled her close. Sylvia tried to keep hold of Elizabeth's hand, but her cousin's slender fingers slipped from her grasp. Elizabeth laughed and kissed Henry's cheek. He murmured something in her ear, and Sylvia was struck by the certainty that she had been entirely forgotten.

Unnoticed, she slipped away from the couple and searched out her mother. Mama's face lit up at the sight of her. "I had no idea you were such a fine dancer," she said, pulling Sylvia into a hug.

"Elizabeth taught me." And now that they had shown everyone what Bergstrom girls could do, Elizabeth had returned to Henry. Sylvia had done her best, but anyone could see that Henry was her cousin's favorite dance partner, no matter what she had declared as they practiced in the nursery.

Sylvia climbed onto her mother's lap and watched the dancing for a while, her eyelids drooping. When her mother offered to take her upstairs to bed, Sylvia roused herself and insisted that she meant to stay up until midnight, like everyone else. She went off to find Claudia, who demanded that Sylvia teach her the Charleston. Sylvia showed her the few steps she knew, but dancing with Claudia was not as much fun as performing with Elizabeth, and she soon lost interest. When she spotted Great-Aunt Lucinda carrying a tray of her delicious *Pfannkuchen* to the dessert table, she hurried over and took two of the delicious jelly-filled doughnuts. Licking sugar from her fingertips, she considered taking a plate to Elizabeth, but her lovely cousin was once again circling the dance floor in Henry's arms. He was not much of a dancer, Sylvia observed spitefully. He knew the steps well enough but he seemed to be going through the motions without a scrap of enjoyment. But Elizabeth was having a wonderful time, and Sylvia could not pretend otherwise.

She finished her dessert and went off to find a dance partner. She would show Elizabeth that she, too, could have just as much fun with someone else.

Her father was pleased by her invitation to dance, as was her grandpa after him. Claudia found her and they made up their own dance, holding hands and spinning around in a circle until they became so dizzy they fell down. When they had come too close to crashing into dancing aunts and uncles too many times, their mother begged them to find some other way to amuse themselves. At that moment the musicians took a break, and Great-Aunt Lucinda called everyone to the fireside for *Bleigiessen*. "See what the New Year will bring you," she joked. "Unless you'd rather not know."

Only Grandma, who found fortune-telling unsettling, declined. "I'd rather have another jelly doughnut than a prediction of bad news," she said, settling into a chair near the dessert table, waving off the others' teasing protests that she should not assume that the news would be bad.

Sylvia, who had seen lead pouring on other New Year's Eves, knew that the game would almost certainly promise good fortune to everyone, since the funny shapes were rarely so obvious that the observers could reach only one conclusion. She darted through the crowd and found a seat on the floor close to the fireside. Great-Aunt Lucinda went first, melting a small piece of lead in an old spoon held above the flames. When it had turned to liquid, she poured it into a bowl of water, and everyone bent closer to see what shape the lead would take.

"It looks like a pretzel," Great-Aunt Lydia declared. "You're going to become a baker."

Everyone laughed. "I'm already a baker," said Great-Aunt Lucinda, passing the spoon to a neighbor. Everyone who had ever tried her delicious cookies or apple strudel chimed in their agreement.

One by one family and friends held the spoon over the fire, poured the melted lead into the water, and interpreted the shapes the metal took as it rapidly cooled. Those gathered around broke into cheers and applause when stars or fish promised good luck, when triangles promised financial improvement, or bells heralded good news. They burst into laughter when one elderly widow's lead formed an unmistakable egg shape, announcing the imminent birth of a child. "It must mean a grandchild," she speculated, but that did not stop her friends from teasing her, claiming that if she had tried *Bleigiessen* the previous New Year's Eve, the lead surely would have taken the shape of a mouse, symbolic of a secret love.

When Sylvia's father took a turn, an anchor shape showed that he would find assistance in an emergency. The crowd mulled this over while Aunt Millie took the spoon, for while it was good to know that he would have help in a time of need, it would be better to avoid the emergency altogether. "This *Bleigiessen* isn't very helpful after all," said Aunt Millie as the lead shavings turned to liquid over the fire. "It tells you just enough to worry you, and not enough to steer you clear of trouble." With that, she poured the lead into the bowl of water and exclaimed with delight when the lead sank and hardened into a lopsided cylinder she insisted was a cake.

"That doesn't look like any cake I'd want to taste," said Great-Aunt Lucinda.

"We can't all be bakers, like you," Aunt Millie retorted. "We all know that a cake means a celebration is coming, and of course that must refer to the wedding." With that, she handed the spoon to her future son-in-law.

Sylvia inched forward, holding her breath as Henry melted the lead then shrugged noncommittally as he poured it upon the water. The liquid metal thinned and elongated as it sank to the bottom of the bowl, and a gasp went up from the onlookers as two interlocking rings appeared. Sylvia waited, willing the rings to break, for that meant separation — and perhaps, perhaps, an end to the engagement. She waited, but the rings remained stubbornly joined.

"I've never seen rings form like that," Great-Aunt Lydia breathed. "A single ring alone signifies a wedding. Rings joined in this fashion surely indicate that you two will have a happy, enduring marriage. Congratulations, young man."

Henry's skepticism promptly vanished, and he flashed a grin to his future bride, who beamed and reached for his hand. Sylvia muffled a groan of disgust and snatched up the spoon from the hearth. She hoped for a ball to announce that good luck would roll her way, but instead the figure in the bowl resembled Grandma's eyeglasses. Sylvia scowled as her family debated which of the two possible interpretations to choose, whether she would one day be very wise or very old, and decided that old age was the more likely of the two. "It could be both," she protested, handing the spoon to her sister. "Why not both?" And why did her family — with the exception of her mother and Great-Aunt Lucinda — find it so difficult to believe that Sylvia could one day be wise?

Claudia went next, biting her lip hopefully as she peered into the bowl of water. "What is it?" she asked. "A tree? An arrow? What does it mean?"

"Looks like an ax to me," offered a neighbor.

When Claudia turned to Great-Aunt Lucinda for confirmation, the older woman reluctantly nodded. "It does resemble a hatchet."

"You saw one of those yourself, when we were girls," cried Great-Aunt Lydia. "Oh, but that can't be right. For you, perhaps, but not for pretty little Claudia."

"Thank you, sister dear," said Great-Aunt Lucinda dryly, and when the guests pressed her for an explanation, she held up her hands to quiet them. "Now, now, it's supposed to mean that you'll find disappointment in love, but take heart, Claudia. The fortune is only meant to tell you what the year ahead may bring, not what might happen when you're a grown woman. I don't think you need to worry about being unlucky in love at your age."

Claudia held back tears. "But what if it's not just for the year ahead? What if it's for my whole life?" A few well-meaning women reached out to comfort her, but she shook off their reassurances. "Sylvia won't reach old age in a single year, but that's what her fortune says."

"Many of these symbols have more than one meaning," Aunt Millie reminded her. "Your hatchet must mean something else."

"Maybe you're going to become a lumber-jack," Sylvia suggested.

Claudia glared at her as the adults rocked with laughter. "Make jokes if you want. I don't think this game is fun anymore." She flounced off to join Grandma by the dessert table.

"After that, I'm almost afraid to take a turn," said Elizabeth, reaching for the spoon Claudia had flung down on the hearth. With a quick smile for Henry, she melted a few of the remaining lead shavings and let them fall from the spoon into the water. At first the lead gathered itself up into a ball — "Good luck will roll your way," an onlooker said — but then a dimple appeared along one side, and the opposite edge seemed to flatten.

"A heart," Henry's mother announced, beaming at her future daughter-in-law. "Elizabeth has found true love."

As Elizabeth's face glowed from happiness in the firelight, Sylvia boiled over with impatience. "That's not a heart," she declared. "A heart has a pointed tip. That looks like . . . like a piece of fruit, that's all."

Elizabeth gazed into the bowl, her smile slowly fading. Then she looked up and gave Sylvia a wistful smile. "I suppose you're right." She turned away to gaze into the bowl. "The question is, what sort of fruit, and what does it mean?"

"It looks like an apricot to me," said Great-Aunt Lucinda. "See the slightly elongated shape, and the indentation along the edge? That part could be the stem —"

"It's a heart," said Henry's mother, but less convincingly.

"Maybe it's an orange," said Henry, making his way to the fireside. He offered Elizabeth his hand and helped her to her feet. "An orange ripening on a tree in a grove on a ranch in sunny southern California."

"It's an apple," Sylvia shot back. "It looks exactly like one of the apples we picked from our own trees last autumn."

"Whatever variety of fruit it may be," Sylvia's mother broke in gently, "I think we can all agree on the meaning. For Elizabeth, the year ahead is certain to be sweet and good and flavorful."

All of the adults chimed in their agreement, but Sylvia scowled, pretending not to notice her mother's warning look. The shape was an apple and it meant that Elizabeth ought to stay close to Elm Creek Manor, where she could enjoy the harvest year after year.

Only a few lead shavings remained when Sylvia's mother came forward to try her hand. A few guests who had wandered away from the game returned to the fireside to see what the future held for their beloved hostess. Sylvia saw neighbors exchange glances and overheard their whispers, and her heart swelled with pride. Everyone loved Mama, and everyone wanted her to receive the best fortune of the evening. Sylvia hoped that the lead would take the shape of a cow, which represented healing, and she resolved to call the lump of lead a cow if it even remotely resembled any four-legged animal. If Elizabeth and Henry's mother could interpret the figures liberally to suit themselves, so could she.

Sylvia's mother hesitated before dribbling the melted lead into the bowl of water. A hush fell over the room. Sylvia's mother bent over the bowl, then sat back on her heels and took a deep, shuddering breath. Sylvia inched closer to see, and her stomach suddenly knotted in cold, sickening dread.

The metal had hardened in the shape of a cross. There could be no mistaking it. And crosses signified death.

Someone broke the silence with a low moan, but was quickly hushed. Sylvia's mother looked around at the faces of her friends and family and forced a smile. "Perhaps I should have followed Grandma's example after all," she said, her voice trembling.

"It's just a foolish game," said Great-Aunt Lucinda. "It's not real."

"What's wrong?" said Henry. "That looks like a sign of good fortune to me."

Sylvia balled her hands into fists and glared at him. "Don't you know what crosses mean?" He was so stupid, so stupid!

"That's not a cross." Henry bent over the bowl to scrutinize the figure within, and then straightened, shaking his head. "That second line's too thin and not straight enough. Anyone can see that's a threaded needle. That has to be a good sign for a family full of quilters."

"Of course. I see it now," said Great-Aunt Lucinda quickly. "Perhaps it means you're going to make many quilts this year, Eleanor."

"Or perhaps the meaning is more symbolic," said Elizabeth. "Needles are useful and necessary, just as you are to all of us. Needles can make a home warmer and more beautiful. Needles are used for . . . for mending."

Henry put his arm around Elizabeth's shoulders, but his eyes were on Sylvia's mother. "Looks like you'll be doing some mending in the year ahead, Mrs. Bergstrom."

An inflection he gave the word suggested healing rather than darning socks or repairing little girls' torn hems. Sylvia's mother trembled with another deep breath, but then she offered Henry a warm, grateful smile. "Of course. I see it now." She reached out a hand, and Henry and Elizabeth helped her to her feet. "I do hope this doesn't mean I have to rush off to my sewing basket until after the party."

A ripple of laughter went through the crowd, but Sylvia caught the undercurrent of sadness. Her mother must have heard it, too, for she turned a brilliant smile on her loved ones and gestured to the musicians to strike up another tune. As the first merry notes sounded, Sylvia's father was at Mama's side, inviting her to dance.

Sylvia no longer felt like dancing. She wished that she had come up with the new interpretation of the symbol her mother had seen in the water, wished that she had been the one to protect her mother from the bleak foretelling, the one to bask in the warmth of her mother's grateful smile. And yet she felt oddly grateful to Henry for speaking up when she and everyone else had been paralyzed with foreboding. As much as she disliked him, she was glad he had been there.

Now, if only he would go home.

Sylvia curled up in an armchair and watched the couples circle the dance floor like snowflakes in a storm — her mother resting her cheek on her father's chest, Elizabeth gazing lovingly up at Henry. They danced on, not knowing what the year ahead held in store, but determined to face the best of times and the worst of times together.

Sylvia's mother did not die in the year to come, but her weak heart did not mend itself as they all prayed it miraculously would. She had always been the peacemaker of the family, so perhaps the mending the symbol foretold was the gentling of arguments and the soothing of hurt feelings within the family circle. Or perhaps the lead shape had carried a simpler, more literal meaning, for Sylvia's mother, like all the women of the family, sewed furiously that winter, making quilts, a trousseau, and a beautiful wedding gown for Elizabeth.

For Sylvia's beloved cousin did not come to her senses as Sylvia hoped, but married Henry and left Elm Creek Manor for a ranch in southern California. Whether Elizabeth had indeed found her true love, or only oranges and apricots, Sylvia never knew, for as the years passed, letters from Triumph Ranch appeared in their mailbox less frequently until they finally stopped coming.

Sylvia's mother saw four more New Years come and go, until she finally succumbed to death quietly at home, with her loved ones around her. Doctors had been predicting her death since childhood, but no amount of time would have been enough to prepare themselves for life without her. On that dark day, they thought only of their loss, and no one remembered the lead cross she had seen in the water.

If Claudia remembered the dire prediction she had received that New Year's Eve, she never spoke of it. As a pretty and popular young woman, she enjoyed the admiration of all the young men of the Elm Creek Valley and seemed, for a time, to have escaped the unhappy fate the lead figure in the water had foretold. Her disappointment in love came many years later, after the war, after her marriage to the man whose cowardice led to the deaths of Sylvia's husband and their younger brother. This was the great betrayal that had compelled Sylvia to abandon the family home, the breach no apology could heal.

As for the eyeglasses Sylvia had seen in the bowl of water, she did indeed achieve a ripe old age. Whether she had attained wisdom as well — that was another thing altogether. She certainly had not attained it in time to reconcile with Claudia before her death. Whenever Sylvia reflected back upon that New Year's Eve, she could not help but wonder whether the hatchet had warned not only of Claudia's unhappy marriage but also of the severing of ties between two sisters.

If ever Sylvia needed wisdom, she needed it now. She sighed and ran a hand over the quilt top, pausing to study the changes she had made to three of the Mother's Favorite blocks. For one, she had substituted a Hatchet block to remind her of the fortune Claudia had cast that long-ago winter night. A True Lover's Knot in the center of another block called to mind her parents, who had loved each other like no other man and woman Sylvia had ever known. Another block boasted an Orange Peel pattern, which Sylvia had sewn as a tribute to Elizabeth and Henry. She hoped they had been blessed with true love and all the sweetness life had to offer. How she wished she had not been so selfish, so jealous of their blossoming affection. If only she had understood that in loving Henry, Elizabeth had not depleted her heart's store of love. There had always been enough left over for her favorite little cousin. Had Sylvia not tried to keep Elizabeth's love all for herself, perhaps Elizabeth would have stayed in touch with the family. Perhaps Sylvia would know what had become of her, and why her letters from Triumph Ranch had stopped coming.

Sylvia and Andrew drove on, leaving the rolling, forested hills of Pennsylvania behind them. Sylvia had always considered herself a reasonable person, sensible and not given to superstitious flights of fancy, and yet she could not help wondering if Henry had a hand in her current predicament. She could not miss the similarities between his situation and that which she now faced, and she suspected he would be amused, if he were still alive, to witness her current predicament. Now, at long last, she understood how he had felt, how Elizabeth had felt, when confronted with Sylvia's foolish objections to their wedding. Now, too late for it to do any good, she understood how it must have pained Elizabeth that Sylvia had withheld her blessing.

On that New Year's Eve so long ago, a more reasonable child might have chosen to mend her ways and make a new start with Henry, as befitting the New Year. Not Sylvia. A few days into the New Year, she resumed her silly pranks with renewed determination to prevent the wedding. She hid Aunt Millie's scissors so that she could not work on the wedding gown, but Aunt Millie simply borrowed Great-Aunt Lucinda's. She stole the keys to Elizabeth's red steamer trunk and flung them into Elm Creek so that her cousin could not pack her belongings. She refused to try on her flower girl dress no matter how the aunts wheedled and coaxed, until they were forced to make a pattern from the frock she had worn on Christmas. She even came right out and told Henry that she and everyone else in the family hated him, but Henry did not believe her, and he did not go away until he took Elizabeth with him to California.

Just as Andrew's children misjudged Sylvia, so had she misjudged Henry. She had seen him through the filter of a young girl's jealousy and had never considered that he might cherish Elizabeth and bring her joy. On that New Year's Eve, when he had turned foreboding into hope by imagining another future for her mother, Sylvia had been offered a glimpse of the man he truly was, a man of kindness, reassurance, and generosity of spirit. If only she'd had the sense to be grateful that her beloved cousin had found such a partner.

Could she hope for more from Andrew's children than she had been willing to give? If Andrew's children never accepted their marriage, wasn't it precisely what she deserved, a just punishment for her own selfishness so long ago?

Perhaps. She could not deny it. But Andrew had done nothing wrong. He deserved better even if Sylvia did not.

Two days in New York awaited them, two days to savor the Christmas season in the city, alight with anticipation of the New Year. Sylvia intended to enjoy their honeymoon, but she would also make time to complete her quilt before they continued east to Amy's home in Hartford, Connecticut.

She would find out soon if Amy possessed the insight that had eluded Sylvia as a child.

CHAPTER TWO

Sylvia continued to sew down the binding as she and Andrew drove across New Jersey, but she put the quilt away as they approached the Lincoln Tunnel. Soon they had arrived in Manhattan, where a light flurry of snow whirled down upon the mini-van from a clear blue sky. Sylvia clasped her hands in her lap in girlish delight as they drove through Midtown, passed Central Park, and turned onto East 62nd Street on the Upper East Side. She had not been to the city in many years, and it seemed new and familiar all at the same time. She considered it a stroke of good fortune that they found a parking spot not far from their bed and breakfast inn, a five-story brownstone called the 1863 House. One of the proprietors was a regular guest at Elm Creek Quilt Camp, and every year she urged Sylvia and Andrew to come stay with them anytime they were in New York. "It's the least I can do to repay your hospitality," she said. "Your classes inspire me, and Elm Creek Manor restores my soul. Where would I be without you?"

Adele, who had retired from a successful career on Wall Street in her mid-forties to pursue quilting and other artistic interests, was given to such dramatic statements, so Sylvia was at first not convinced that she was meant to take the offer seriously. But when Adele repeated the invitation in a Christmas card Sylvia received just after she and Andrew had decided to move up their wedding date, she finally accepted.

Since the newlyweds had set their Christmas Eve wedding date only a week ahead of time, they did not expect Adele and her husband, Julius, to have a room available on such short notice. Andrew even suggested they stay in a large chain hotel rather than impose on their generosity, but Sylvia had faith in Adele and suggested they at least inquire. A bed and breakfast in one of the finest neighborhoods in the city would be much more charming than an impersonal hotel room, and Sylvia couldn't bear to pass up the opportunity to see firsthand the historic inn she had caught glimpses of in the amusing stories Adele had shared at quilt camp.

In a stroke of good fortune, although the 1863 House was usually fully booked through the Christmas season, a last-minute cancellation had freed up what Adele promised was one of their most charming rooms. "Don't overbook yourself during your stay," Adele warned. "I promised the staff of the City Quilter I'd bring you by if you ever came to town." Sylvia rarely turned down an invitation to browse through fabric bolts and admire ingenious new quilting gadgets, so she happily agreed to leave plenty of time to visit Manhattan's best quilt shop.

Adele was off at the market when they arrived, but Julius welcomed them and showed them to the Garden Room on the first floor. The former drawing room boasted a twelve-foot ceiling and a large, south-facing bow window with lace curtains that made the most of the winter sunlight. French doors led to a private terrace garden, dusted with late December snow, and a mahogany wardrobe stood beside a marble fireplace with an elegantly carved wooden mantel. Along the near wall, a striking, multicolored scrap quilt adorned a grand four-poster bed. Sylvia quickly set her suitcase down and went to examine it. "This isn't one of Adele's creations," she remarked, noting the antique fabric prints and colors. The block design resembled the Thousand Pyramids pattern, with four corner triangles composed of thirty-six smaller triangles separated by rectangular sashing arranged around a small, cheddar-yellow Sawtooth Star.

"It's one of Adele's favorite discoveries," Julius confirmed. "She insisted we bring it out for you to use in honor of your wedding. Adele said she could think of no one who would appreciate it more."

Delighted, Sylvia ran her hand over the bright, scrappy top. Adele had indeed discovered a treasure. The fabrics indicated that it dated from the latter third of the eighteenth century, but its excellent condition belied its age. Someone must have cherished this quilt, for it had been given the gentlest of care.

"I imagine this quilt has quite a story to tell," she murmured, thinking of the unknown quiltmaker who had spent months, perhaps years, sewing the tiny triangles together by hand.

"I'll bet this house does, too," said Andrew admiringly, resting his hand on the carved mantelpiece.

"The quilt's provenance is somewhat uncertain, as it is for so many antiques," said Julius. "But Adele and I would be glad to tell you what we know about the house over dinner tonight, unless you have other plans?"

They had tickets for a popular Broadway musical that one of Andrew's old buddies from his army days had managed to get for them. ("His daughter has connections," Andrew had explained when Sylvia marveled at their good fortune. "She's going with a fellow who works in the ticket office.") An early dinner with their proprietors would suit them perfectly. They arranged to meet later that afternoon, and Julius returned to his work while Sylvia and Andrew unpacked.

With a few hours to spare before dinner, Sylvia and Andrew decided to stroll along the Museum Mile to stretch their legs after the long drive, enjoy the sights and sounds of the city, and make plans for the rest of their visit. The air was brisk, but not unbearably so, and the wind was light enough that Sylvia's wool coat, scarf, and mittens warded off the cold. "Should we take advantage of the after Christmas sales?" she teased, tucking her arm through Andrew's as shoppers hurried past with bags from Bergdorf Goodman and FAO Schwarz. She laughed at her husband's disconcerted expression as he struggled to find a good excuse to refuse. She knew that the afternoon of shopping he had promised her was not his favorite item on the honeymoon itinerary.

At four o'clock, they circled back and met Adele and Julius at Mon Petit Café, a charming bistro only steps away from the 1863 House. Adele greeted Sylvia with a warm embrace. "Such a lovely bride," she exclaimed, and told Andrew that he was a lucky man. Andrew proudly agreed, but a wry twist to his smile told Sylvia that he did not expect to receive such a resounding endorsement at the next stop on their honeymoon tour.

Inside the bistro, a low murmur of voices and the aromas of roasting meats and spices warmed the air. Their table near the window offered a sunny view of Lexington Avenue, but Adele's irrepressible joy diverted Sylvia's attention from the sights outside. She seemed about to burst with a happy secret, and Sylvia hid a smile, knowing that her expressive, demonstrative friend would not be able to keep them in suspense for long.

Andrew, a quintessential steak-and-potatoes man, at first looked askance at the menu when he saw the French names for each dish. Just as the waiter appeared, he brightened and ordered Steak Frites —

which as far as Sylvia could discern, was French for steak and fries. Since one of them ought to be daring, she chose Magret de Canard, roast duck breast in raspberry coulis with wild rice, even though she had only tried duck once and had no idea what a coulis was. "Don't tell me," she said when Julius began to explain. "I want to be surprised. Perhaps that should be my New Year's resolution: to take more chances and seek out more surprises."

"That's my resolution every year," said Adele, raising her wine glass in a toast to herself.

"It's worked well for you so far," remarked Julius. "Think of all you've accomplished because you're willing to take chances. We should all have your courage."

"You make me sound much braver than I am," Adele protested, but her smile thanked him.

When Sylvia and Andrew urged them to explain, Adele reminded Sylvia of how she had once had a lucrative career as a stockbroker. "I was successful by most people's standards. I had a corner office, great salary, all the perks — but I was working eighty-hour weeks. I had no time for my friends. I gobbled all my meals on the run. I read stock reports on the treadmill at the gym and answered cell phone calls in the bathroom. You laugh, but I'm serious. I was always working. It never stopped."

"Just imagining it wears me out," said Andrew.

"It wore me out, too," Adele confessed. "But whenever thoughts of slowing down or taking a vacation crossed my mind, I drove them away. I had always pushed myself beyond other peoples' expectations, and to stop doing so would be a sign of weakness, or worse yet, some kind of moral failing. I couldn't let myself down."

"I don't know who she was doing it all for," Julius confided to the older couple. "She makes it sound like she was under constant scrutiny and judgment, but I've always believed that people are far too wrapped up in their own concerns to pay much attention to others' struggles."

"For better or for worse, that does seem to be the case," admitted Sylvia, although she could have shared many personal anecdotes of small-town life to the contrary.

"I don't blame anyone but myself for the pressure I felt in those days," Adele said. "All around me were colleagues with the same responsibilities, long hours, and stresses I had, but they were thriving. They enjoyed waging the daily wars. It took me a long time to admit to myself that I wasn't happy. But I didn't know what to do. I didn't know how to stop without giving up, without admitting defeat."

Sylvia nodded, although she did not see how leaving a miserable job could be construed as admitting defeat. There was far more virtue to be found in diverting from a course that clearly wasn't working than in plodding down a road one knew led to a bad end.

"So I went through the motions." Adele sighed and toyed with her fork. "And then came September eleventh."

When she fell silent, Andrew gently asked, "Did you lose loved ones?"

"I don't know anyone who didn't. I lost several friends that day, acquaintances I knew through work, clients —" Adele took a deep breath. "There are no words. There just aren't any words for it."

Her listeners nodded.

"Adele also lost her home when the Towers collapsed," said Julius.

"Oh, dear," said Sylvia. "I had no idea. You never mentioned it."

"My apartment building was covered with soot and debris," Adele explained. "None of the residents could go home. I stayed with a friend — slept on her sofa, tried to figure out what to do next. Weeks passed before we were allowed to return for some belongings. Everything I owned was covered in a thick, white shroud of dust. I threw a few salvageable things into a bag and never looked back. It was hard to care about *things* when so many innocent people had lost their lives."

Sylvia reached out and patted her hand. "I understand, dear."

"I had long since returned to work. After all that had happened, it seemed trivial to brood over my dissatisfaction with my career. My feelings hadn't changed; I just stopped thinking of them as important enough to act upon. Then one December afternoon, I was out apartment hunting when I passed the 1863 House."

"She went inside, took a tour, and made an offer within a week, even though she had never run a bed and breakfast in her life," her husband broke in, shaking his head in proud incredulity.

"It didn't happen quite that quickly," Adele said, laughing. "I did my due diligence. I made a business plan. But if I hadn't seen that quilt in the window, I might still be toiling away on Wall Street."

Sylvia was eager to hear how a quilt had played a role in Adele's story, and she urged her friend to continue. Adele explained that not long before she bought the 1863 House, her therapist had encouraged her to take up a creative hobby — something for pure enjoyment completely unrelated to her job. Since her grandmother had quilted and because at that low point in her life she felt drawn to items of warmth and comfort, she signed up for a beginner's quilting class at the City Quilter.

"I was a newly minted quilter, with all the zeal of a recent convert," said Adele. "When I walked past the brownstone that day, I glimpsed a quilt through the window, a Crazy Quilt draped over the davenport. I wanted a closer look, but rather than risk arrest by peering through the window, I knocked on the door and asked the proprietor if I could come inside for a closer look."

The proprietor was a quilter herself, and so pleased by Adele's interest that she offered to show her all the antique quilts in the inn. One very special quilt she saved for last, withdrawing it from a custom-made, muslin-lined wardrobe in the family's private quarters on the fifth floor.

"It was the quilt I placed on the bed in your suite," Adele said, confirming Sylvia's guess. "Can you imagine sewing together all those tiny triangles by hand? And those fabrics — it's a veritable catalog of mid- to late-nineteenth-century prints. The proprietor unfolded the quilt with such reverence that I had to know why. She told me that the quilt had come with the brownstone when she and her husband bought it forty years before. The previous owners had told her that the quilt was there when they purchased it, too. Intrigued, she traced its ownership as far back as she could and finally concluded that the quilt had probably belonged to the original owners of the house.

"As she returned the quilt to the wardrobe for safekeeping, she remarked that the quilt and the house had been together so long that it would be a shame to part them. She only hoped that whoever bought the house would cherish both quilt and residence as much as she had." Adele smiled. "That's when I knew I had to make an offer."

"Was it the quilt you wanted, or the house?" asked Andrew.

"I couldn't have one without the other," Adele pointed out with a laugh. "I wanted the quilt, sure, but I wanted the house and the life at least as much. Talk about hubris. I didn't think there would be anything to running an inn. Change the sheets every once in a while, take reservations, serve bagels and coffee —" Adele rolled her eyes. "I thought if I could handle Wall Street, I could handle a little B&B. Let's just say I had a very sharp learning curve. But I never regretted it. I closed on the property on the afternoon of New Year's Eve. As I signed the papers, I told myself that 2002 would be my new beginning. No more would I stay in a safe, predictable routine that made me miserable. Predictability is a trap and safety is an illusion. Love and happiness, on the other hand, are real, but you don't find them without taking chances." She smiled at Julius. "Love for my work eventually led to love of another kind."

After she took over the inn, she explained, she wanted to discover all she could about its history. The previous owners shared what they knew, but Adele suspected the former single-family residence had a richer and more intriguing story to tell. Since Hunter College was nearby, she contacted its history department for advice. That phone call led to a meeting with Julius, a professor who had written several books on New York history. They fell in love, and a year later, they married.

By that time Adele had settled into her new career. She loved everything about her new life — meeting people from around the world, sending off her guests each morning with a delicious breakfast, introducing them to intriguing places off the usual tourist track, making them feel like true New Yorkers no matter how brief their stay in the city. When she found the time, she continued to research the history of the lovely old brownstone. With Julius's help, she learned enough about research methods and historical scholarship to qualify for a Master's degree, if only she had been officially enrolled.

Sylvia, who had heard some of Adele's stories at Elm Creek Quilt Camp, said, "I do hope you'll share some of that history with us."

Adele promised she would, and as soon as their delicious meal was finished, they returned to the inn. "The name 1863 House comes from the year the brownstone was built, as I'm sure you've already guessed," she told them as they climbed the front stairs. Inside, she showed them down a long hallway that had been converted to a gallery, displaying framed enlargements of black-and-white illustrations that appeared to be political cartoons. Sylvia recognized caricatures of Jefferson Davis and Robert E. Lee in various states of distress, and others of a somber but noble Abraham Lincoln in metaphorical narratives — sewing a divided nation together, visiting his Southern rivals in their nightmares. Other drawings parodied long-forgotten political figures and controversies, while another seemed to mock the simultaneous efforts of both the North and the South to recruit freed slaves for their armies.

"The man who built this residence was an artist and political activist named John Colcraft," Adele said. "You wouldn't know it from his political cartoons, but he was a South Carolinian by birth."

"I wouldn't have guessed that," Andrew remarked, peering closely at an illustration of a particularly tough-looking Union general wiping his shoes on a map of the Confederate states.

"His family had made its fortune in cotton, and as the second son, John often traveled North on business for his father. On one of those journeys he met a Quaker woman named Harriet Beals, who was born in Chester County, Pennsylvania, to a family of staunch abolitionists. By 1858, John had embraced her faith, renounced slavery, and married her, although not necessarily in that order."

"I've always wondered how a man who owed his livelihood to the exploitation of slave labor managed to win the heart of a dedicated abolitionist," Julius remarked.

"He must have been a fine talker," said Adele, with a glance that suggested she knew another man who fit that description. "Don't forget, he did renounce slavery. He also begged his father to free his slaves, but his father refused and disowned his son. Or the son disowned the father, it isn't entirely clear. John Colcraft later wrote that on that day he had lost his birthright but regained his soul."

"Fine words, indeed," said Sylvia, though her own experiences had made it impossible to consider any familial estrangement without regret, without wondering what might have been.

"The couple settled in Philadelphia for a time, which is where John began his artistic career." Adele led them down the hall at a pace that allowed them to examine the framed cartoons more carefully. "As a Quaker and a pacifist, he battled the evils he saw in the world around him with a pen rather than a sword. He began with innocuous illustrations for a city neighborhood, but as the Civil War approached, his drawings took on a more editorial slant. As his fame — or in certain circles, notoriety — grew, he moved to New York and became a regular artist for *Harper's*."

"Which brought them here," Sylvia guessed, admiring the front room of the house as Adele and Julius led them inside and invited them to sit.

Adele nodded. "At the end of 1862, John received a considerable inheritance from his mother's side of the family — 'untainted by the stain of slavery,' as he put it — and he used it to build this home for Harriet and their two children. They moved into it in the spring of 1863, at a time of rising tensions in the city."

The Emancipation Proclamation had been in force for several months by then, Adele reminded them. Proslavery organizations responded to the increasing political power of abolitionists by warning working-class New Yorkers of the increased competition for laborers' jobs that would inevitably follow should slavery be abolished and the freed slaves move North. A new, stricter draft law only fanned the flames of unrest: Every male citizen between the ages of twenty and thirty-five, as well as all unmarried male citizens between thirty-five and forty-five, were considered eligible for military service and could be chosen for duty by lottery. Certain exceptions could be made, however. If a man could hire a substitute to take his place or if he could pay the federal government a three-hundred-dollar exemption fee, he would not have to serve. African-Americans were not subject to the draft because they were not considered citizens.

Working-class men, who would bear the brunt of the new law, were outraged. "Then, as it would now, the conflict played out in the press," said Adele. "John Colcraft was right in the thick of it, skewering his political opponents and satirizing racism and hypocrisy on both sides." She gestured to the four walls. "His most significant work was created in this very room. That desk is a reproduction of the one he used, based upon his own sketches of the original."

Fear, anger, and racial tensions rose throughout the city as spring turned into summer and the first lottery approached, Adele told them. On July 11, the first names were drawn, and for nearly two days the city remained quiet, holding its breath, waiting to see if the danger had passed. But early in the morning of July 13, the tensions erupted in violence and bloodshed. At first the rioters targeted only military and government buildings, which to them represented all that was unfair about the new conscription process. People were safe from attack as long as they did not attempt to interfere with the mob's destruction. Before long, however, the rioting took an uglier, more sinister turn as the long-simmering racial tensions finally boiled over. Mobs began attacking African-American residents, their businesses, and any other symbol of black community, culture, or political power.

"Even children were not safe," said Adele. "A mob armed with clubs and bats descended upon the Colored Orphan Asylum at Fifth and Forty-Second, where more than two hundred children lived. They looted the place of anything of value — food, clothing, bedding — and then they burned down the building."

"They attacked an orphanage?" gasped Sylvia. "Had they no shame?"

"What happened to the children?" asked Andrew.

"The building was a total loss," said Adele. "Somehow the matron, superintendent, and a handful of volunteers managed to get all the children outside unharmed — but the mob was still there, destroying property, attacking and even killing African-Americans unlucky enough to fall into their hands. The superintendent split the children into two groups to try to lead them through the rioting to safety. Two hundred and thirty-three children followed the matron and superintendent to the police station at Thirty-Fifth Street. The remaining twenty-nine made their way here under Harriet Beals Colcraft's protection."

"For five days this house was their sanctuary," Julius added. "For five days the children were sheltered in these rooms while the worst atrocities you can imagine were carried out in the streets."

"I'd prefer to only imagine them, if you please," said Sylvia, when Julius seemed prepared to describe those horrors with a historian's eye for detail.

"While Harriet cared for the children, she must have been out of her mind with worry," said Adele. "She had led the orphans to an empty house. John had gone out, perhaps to the newspaper office to check on the safety of friends, perhaps to witness the events unfold so he could draw about them later. Only after the rioting subsided did Harriet receive word that her husband was in the hospital. He had been discovered unconscious and badly beaten on the waterfront, where white longshoremen were attacking black dockworkers and sailors. He must have come between the two sides."

"Or a political enemy recognized him and took advantage of the uproar and confusion to exact some personal revenge," said Julius. "That's my pet theory, anyway."

"I think it's more likely he rushed to a victim's aid only to fall prey to the attackers himself," said Adele. "He never fully recovered from his injuries, but suffered pain and difficulty walking for the rest of his life. He considered it a blessing that his attackers had struck him on the back and legs and left his arms unscathed so he could still draw, and therefore could still support his family."

"Some blessing," said Andrew. "If they had tried to hit him but missed, well, *that* I'd call a blessing."

"Adele has been entertaining her guests with stories of the Colcraft family ever since," said Julius. "Almost every time, at the end of the tale, one of her listeners will say, 'You should write a book.' "

"I was going to make that suggestion myself," remarked Sylvia. "The Colcrafts certainly experienced an interesting chapter of New York history, and you have a gift for words."

"I thought about it," said Adele. "Julius has written two books for university presses, and I've lost count of how many articles he's written for academic journals, so I knew something of the publication process. I wanted to tell the Colcrafts' story, but the thought of writing a book was so daunting. I couldn't imagine tackling such an enormous project. And what if I couldn't finish? Or what if I did finish and no one cared? What if every publisher in the world rejected it? What if the writing turned out to be one big waste of time?"

"She found every logical reason not to try," said Julius. "I tried to encourage her, but —" He shook his head ruefully. "Why listen to me? I'm just her husband."

"Then last Christmas my mother gave me a book on New York history," said Adele. "It seems like the perfect gift for a history buff, doesn't it?"

"It made her miserable," said Julius.

"But don't ever tell my mother," Adele warned them. "She doesn't know. Anyway, for a few days after Christmas I alternated between reading chapters of the book and moping around the inn in a brood. Whenever our guests couldn't overhear, I complained to Julius about relevant historical details omitted from the book, other sources that the author should have consulted, and conclusions that didn't fit the historical record. Again and again I asked, 'How can this guy get his book published and I can't?'

"Finally, Julius must have heard enough, because he retorted, 'How? By having the courage to actually sit down and write his book, and send it out into the world so that people like you could stew in jealousy and gripe about how you could have done better.' "

"You said that?" Andrew asked Julius. "How many nights did you have to sleep on the sofa afterward?"

"Not long," said Julius. "Less than a week."

"Oh, don't believe him," said Adele, laughing. "I knew he was right. And yes, I had been duly chastened. But the task of sitting down and writing an entire book was still too overwhelming to contemplate. Then I had a revelation: I didn't have to write the entire book in one sitting."

Everyone laughed.

"That might seem obvious to you," said Adele, "and anyone else with common sense, but it wasn't something I had consciously considered before. Finally I realized that the only way I would ever be a published writer was if I sat down and wrote something."

"That *is* an important part of the process," said Julius, his mouth quirking in a grin.

"I had to push thoughts of failure out of my mind," said Adele. "I told myself that even if I never published my book, it was important to record all I had learned about the Colcrafts and the history of this wonderful brownstone. I was sure our guests would enjoy learning what my research had uncovered, even if no publisher thought the story was worth putting on bookstore shelves. So I made a New Year's resolution: Every day I had to sit down and write a few sentences. I stopped thinking about writing an entire book and instead just focused on those few sentences each day."

"Did you keep your resolution?" asked Sylvia.

"Even on weekends and holidays," said Julius proudly, with an affectionate smile for his wife.

"Running the B&B was still my first love, and I have high standards, so it wasn't easy to find writing time," said Adele. "But I managed. As the weeks passed, I accumulated more and more pages, I wrote for longer stretches of time, and my confidence increased. I was doing it. I was actually writing my book, something I feared I could never do."

"She printed out one copy for each guest room in the inn and had them spiral bound," said Julius. "Our guests read the book, and loved it, and some even asked for autographed copies to take home."

"I had Julius read through the manuscript before I made the guests' copies," Adele hastened to add. "I wanted some editorial oversight, at least. I do have my pride."

"One day, one of our guests asked Adele if she minded if he showed her book to a friend who worked for a publisher," said Julius. "By that time Adele had been sending the manuscript around to literary agents, and had even submitted it to a few contests, but received only rejection letters in reply."

"That was a fun time," said Adele dryly. "Our guest's offer was the first real glimmer of hope I'd seen. Did I mind if he showed it to his friend? Was he crazy? I would have driven him to his friend's office and watched him personally deliver the manuscript if I hadn't thought that would seem too desperate. If I had known that his friend was a senior editor at New York University Press, I might have been too terrified to let him do it, so it's a good thing he didn't mention that until he was on his way out the door with the manuscript in his briefcase."

"Please do tell me that this story has a happy ending," said Sylvia, remembering how upon meeting her friend at the restaurant, she had strongly suspected that Adele was concealing a secret. Now Sylvia was certain she knew why.

A smile lit up Adele's face. "My book is coming out next fall."

Sylvia and Andrew cheered and embraced her, offering their congratulations and promising to buy copies for all of their friends. "It's not going to be a best-seller," warned Adele. "I'm just hoping it will do well locally and in academic bookstores and libraries."

"Don't downplay your success," Sylvia admonished her. "What a wonderful achievement. I'm sure the Colcrafts would be proud."

"All this came about because of a New Year's resolution," Andrew marveled.

"A New Year's resolution that I kept," Adele emphasized. "Anyone can make promises. The challenge is in following through."

They peppered Adele with questions about her forthcoming book until Julius glanced at the clock and reminded them of the time. With a start, Sylvia remembered their theater tickets. She and Andrew hurried off to the Garden Room to dress, and before long, they were on their way.

Sylvia gazed out of the cab window, drinking in the beauty of the city at night and reflecting upon all that Adele had shared with them. Sylvia admired her resolve and her determination to put aside her fears and find a more fulfilling path. Sylvia had made a similar choice not long ago, when she accepted a challenge from a young friend, Sarah McClure, and transformed her family estate into a quilters' retreat. Embarking upon that journey had been a risk, the most significant chance she had taken in decades, but at that point in her life, she'd had very little to lose. She wondered how her life might have been different if, like Adele, she had taken measures to change her life years earlier, and not waited for her sister's death to return home to Elm Creek Manor. If only on one lonely New Year's Eve she had made a resolution as Adele had done, and had come home to ask forgiveness instead of waiting for Claudia to apologize first.

Resolving to start a New Year with a vow to mend broken ties with her sister never occurred to her, Sylvia thought ruefully as their cab pulled on to Broadway. Even if it had, Claudia would not have responded well to the gesture. The sisters had a fractious history when it came to New Year's resolutions, and as much as Sylvia wanted to blame Claudia for that particular conflict, at her ruthlessly honest core, she knew she was at fault.

Sylvia was six years old when her mother

and father announced that a new baby brother or sister would be joining the family in the coming winter. Sylvia was torn between delight over the exciting news and worry for her mother's health. On more than one occasion, she had heard her father gently admonish her mother for overexerting herself. He was always encouraging her to rest, to sit down with some quilting or a book instead of chasing around after her daughters. Her mother tried to accept his suggestions graciously, but Sylvia saw her mouth tighten even as she allowed her husband to help her into an overstuffed chair. Sylvia knew that a baby meant sleepless nights and busy days, and she resolved to help her mother care for the baby so that she could get the rest Sylvia's father and old Dr. Granger insisted she needed.

Sylvia would even willingly change diapers, something Claudia had already confided that she would never do. "Babies are stinky and noisy and they cry all the time," Claudia warned. "Mama and Father will spend all their time with the baby and we'll only get what's left over. You wait and see."

Her sister's warnings filled Sylvia with apprehension, but she brushed them aside when she realized that no one else in the family said such things and that Claudia delivered her dire pronouncements only when she and Sylvia were alone. When the adults of the family were around, Claudia was all smiles and cheerfulness and eagerness to help care for the precious little newborn. The aunts and uncles praised her and called her a good girl whenever she went on in that way, but Sylvia, who secretly hoped for a brother, knew what her sister was up to. Claudia wanted to be the best big sister the Bergstrom family had ever seen only because she had to be the best at everything, not because she really wanted to help, and definitely not because she liked babies. As far as Sylvia could tell, Claudia couldn't stand them.

That was one reason why Sylvia was especially annoyed when Claudia suggested they make a quilt for the baby. Sylvia agreed, wishing she had thought of it first. Sylvia was the better quilter, but Claudia was two years older, so she declared herself in charge of the project. When Sylvia balked, Claudia threw up her hands in frustration. "Fine," she snapped. "I'll make my own quilt for the baby."

Not about to be outdone, Sylvia announced that she would make her own quilt for the baby, too. The argument escalated as they fought over whose quilt the baby would use first, until their voices became so loud that Mama came to investigate. "It's lovely that you want to make a quilt to welcome the baby," she said, short of breath, settling herself carefully into a chair. "But you don't have much time. You'll have to work together if you hope to finish before the baby comes."

She smiled to conceal her weariness, but a stab of guilt reminded Sylvia that their mother needed peace and quiet. Only for her sake did Sylvia agree to work with her sister on a single quilt. At their mother's prompting, they agreed that Sylvia could select the block pattern and Claudia the colors. Sylvia chose the Bear's Paw, a pretty block that even Claudia could not mess up too badly, since it had no curves or set-in pieces. She imagined cuddling Mama's new baby within its soft folds, but Claudia's next words spoiled her contentment: "For colors, I want pink and white, with a little bit of green."

Sylvia protested that those colors would do fine for a baby sister but not for a little boy. "It's a baby. It won't care," said Claudia, rolling her eyes at her sister's ignorance.

"If he's a boy he'll care. Let's pick something else."

"You picked the pattern. I get to pick the

colors. You can't pick everything."

Mama broke in before the argument could become heated. "Compromise, girls."

One glance at her mother's beloved face, tired and disappointed, compelled Sylvia to swallow her pride. "Okay," she told her sister. "You pick the pattern and I'll pick the colors."

Claudia considered only a moment. "Then I pick Turkey Tracks."

Sylvia couldn't believe what she was hearing. Could there be any worse choice for a baby quilt? Not only was it unlikely that Claudia could manage the difficult pattern, but every Bergstrom quilter had heard Grandma's foreboding stories about the pattern once better known as Wandering Foot. A boy given a Wandering Foot quilt would never be content to stay in one place, but would forever be restless, roaming the world, never settling down; a girl would be doomed to an even worse fate, so bleak that Grandma refused to elaborate. "Some people think that by changing a block's name, you get rid of the bad luck," Grandma had once said, watching over Sylvia as she practiced quilting a Nine-Patch. "I know that bad luck isn't so easily fooled."

Sylvia knew it would be far better to give a boy a pink quilt than to give any baby a quilt full of bad luck, but her mother and sister dismissed her concerns and told her not to be upset by foolish superstitions. Against the two of them, united, there was nothing Sylvia could do but select her lucky colors, blue and yellow, and hope for the best.

If anything proved that Claudia was not a responsible, loving elder sister, her insistence upon that quilt pattern should have done so. Why had Claudia insisted upon that bad-luck block instead of choosing from among her favorites? Was she only trying to annoy Sylvia, as she so often did, or was she deliberately wishing her new sibling misfortune?

Despite Sylvia's reluctance, they finished the quilt in two months. Her mother's proud smile as she draped the blue-and-yellow quilt over the cradle filled Sylvia with warmth and happiness, easing her worries. If Mama said everything was all right, if Mama thought the quilt was not to be feared, then surely it must be so.

The weeks passed and their mother's slight figure grew rounder, but only around her tummy. Her limbs were thin and pale, her face shadowed. Sylvia woke one morning to find that Dr. Granger had been summoned in the night. Mama was all right,

Great-Aunt Lucinda assured her, but the doctor had ordered her to remain in bed until the baby was born. Great-Aunt Lucinda made the girls promise not to play loudly in the house, and not to trouble their mother with any unpleasantness. "If ever we needed you two girls to get along, this would be the time," she said with a sigh. "Try not to argue, but if you must, please do it in whispers. Outside."

"What if it's snowing?" asked Claudia. "What if it's dark?"

"I don't care if it's a blizzard at midnight. If you're so angry at your sister that you must express it or burst, take it outside to the barn."

After Great-Aunt Lucinda hurried away to their mother's bedroom, Claudia whirled upon Sylvia. "Did you hear that? You'd better behave yourself." She trotted off after Great-Aunt Lucinda without waiting for a reply.

Sylvia gritted her teeth, balled her hands into fists, and stalked upstairs to the nursery, sick with anger and worry. The baby was not supposed to come until the middle of January, which meant that Mama had to stay in bed a whole month. She would miss Christmas and New Year's Eve. Sylvia did not know what might happen if Mama disebeyed the doctor's orders — she dared not ask — but she could imagine the worst. This time Mama must listen to Father and rest.

No matter how Claudia provoked her, Sylvia would not shout and argue. She would let Claudia have her way and the last word in every discussion if she had to hold her own mouth shut with her hands. Until the baby was born and Mama was allowed out of bed, Sylvia would be the perfect daughter her mother deserved.

For the first few days, Sylvia stuck to her vow so diligently that her father asked her if she felt all right and Great-Aunt Lydia often frowned and felt her forehead as if she believed only illness could subdue Sylvia's naughtiness. Claudia glared at her, suspicious, but was apparently unwilling to be the one to break the tentative truce. Sylvia tried to make her newfound obedience less obvious, but she couldn't help feeling annoyed by the attention her good behavior drew. Did everyone really believe she was ordinarily so naughty that a few quiet days made such a difference?

At first Sylvia's mother submitted to the doctor's orders without complaint, but after a week, she grew restless and bored. One morning, Sylvia passed by her parents' bedroom door and overheard her mother telling her father that she felt strong enough to leave bed. She longed to sit on the front porch, watch the snow fall, and breathe deeply of cold, fresh winter air. "As long as I rest, it shouldn't matter if I'm in bed or in a chair," she said. "Dr. Granger didn't mean for us to take his suggestion so literally."

"It was an order, not a suggestion, and you can ask him to be more specific on his next visit." Sylvia's father tucked the bedcovers around his wife, but she impatiently flung them off again. "Until then, we're going to assume that 'bed rest' means 'rest in bed.' "

"I'll come back straight away if I feel so much as a twinge of pain."

"By then it might be too late. Think of all those stairs. Darling, think of the baby."

Sylvia recognized that tone in her father's voice and knew her mother had lost the argument before it began. Sylvia's mother must have sensed that, too, but she persisted until she had persuaded her husband to allow her more visits with the children. Delighted, the sisters agreed to all of their great-aunts' conditions: no arguing, no loud voices, no bad news, and no complaints. They could read to their mother, or sew, or tell amusing stories, or take her meals on trays. They could not stay too long, only one of them could visit at a time so they did not overtire her, and under no circumstances were they to ask her to get out of bed and play.

Every morning the girls raced downstairs to the kitchen so they could be the first to offer to take Mama her breakfast, knowing she would let them linger until it was time to go to school. Sylvia usually reached the kitchen a few steps ahead of her sister, but Claudia would remind everyone that she was the eldest and more responsible, Sylvia more prone to knocking over her milk at the table and running in the halls. Sylvia protested, but most mornings she sat down glumly to her own breakfast at the kitchen table while her sister glided off bearing the tray without so much as rattling a single dish. Sylvia longed for her to trip on a loose floorboard and send teacup and oatmeal flying through the air, but old Great-Grandfather Hans had built the house too well for that.

Sometimes after school, Sylvia was allowed to take the mail up to her mother and stay to read aloud from one of her schoolbooks or talk about her day. On the last day before school holidays began, Sylvia raced upstairs with an envelope bearing a New

York postmark. It could only be from Grandmother Lockwood, her mother's mother. Grandfather Lockwood had died before Sylvia was born, but he had been a very successful businessman and had founded the most prestigious department store on Fifth Avenue. None of the Lockwoods had ever visited Elm Creek Manor and the Bergstroms never went to New York, except when Father or one of the uncles traveled on business, so the Bergstrom girls had never met anyone from their mother's side of the family. It was probably too far to travel, Sylvia speculated, or Mama was too tired or Grandmother Lockwood too old.

Sylvia was certain the letter would lift her mother's spirits, but instead of tearing open the envelope, her mother turned it over in her hands, felt its thickness, and traced the postmark with a fingertip.

"Aren't you going to read it?" Sylvia asked.

"Not now." Mama smiled briefly and set the letter on the nightstand. "Later. I'd rather hear about your day. How was school? Did you learn anything interesting? Did anyone do anything that made you laugh?"

Sylvia sat down on the edge of the bed and happily told her nearly every detail of all that she had done and seen since leaving the house that morning. A few days later, when she saw the envelope tucked into a book at her mother's bedside, she wondered what news Grandmother Lockwood had sent from New York. Probably nothing terribly interesting, she decided, or her mother would have mentioned it. Grandmother Lockwood didn't work or quilt, and although she used to go to lots of parties when Grandfather Lockwood was alive, as far as Sylvia could discern from the few details Mama had shared through the years, all that concerned her these days was the weather and her health. She no longer lived in the house where Sylvia's mother had grown up, so she wouldn't have any gossip about neighbors and old friends to pass along, either. Still, it was a letter from family, so it must have been a welcome distraction from boring bed rest. Sylvia couldn't wait until the baby came and everything could return to normal.

Christmas approached. Great-Aunt Lydia and Grandma made the famous Bergstrom apple strudel as gifts for the neighbors, and Great-Aunt Lucinda kept the Santa Claus cookie jar filled with her delicious German cookies — *Lebkuchen, Anisplätzchen,* and *Zimtsterne.* Sylvia ached to see her mother among the other women of the family in the warm, fragrant kitchen, kneading strudel dough, peeling apples, laughing, gossiping, and reminiscing about holidays past. The conversations were more subdued that year, the laughter less frequent, as if no one felt like celebrating without Mama in the room. She was the gentle, loving center of every family gathering, and even though she was only upstairs, her absence was sorely felt.

On Christmas morning, Sylvia left Claudia in the ballroom marveling at the presents Santa had left beneath the tree and stole away to the kitchen. Great-Aunt Lucinda glanced through the doorway as if expecting Claudia to follow close behind, and when she didn't, Great-Aunt Lucinda asked Sylvia in a conspiratorial whisper if she wanted to carry Mama's breakfast up to her. Sylvia agreed with a quick nod, afraid that Claudia would overhear and come running to snatch the tray from her hands.

Cautiously she made her way upstairs to her mother's bedroom, torn between determination not to drop a single crumb and worry that if she did not move quickly enough, the tea would cool before she reached the top of the stairs. To her relief, the teacup was still hot to the touch when she reached her mother's bedroom. She took a deep breath and nudged the door open with her foot.

"Breakfast time, Mama," said Sylvia as cheerfully as she could, taken aback by the sight of her mother lying still and pale against the pillows. Was this how she looked every morning upon waking? Had she slept at all?

As her mother smiled and sat up awkwardly, Sylvia set the tray on the nightstand and hurried to assist her. "It's apple strudel and tea," she said, although her mother could surely see that for herself. To cover her embarrassment, Sylvia smiled, tucked the quilt around her mother, and placed the tray on her lap.

"It wouldn't feel like Christmas morning without the famous Bergstrom apple strudel." Mama took a small bite and closed her eyes, savoring the spicy sweetness and the delicate pastry. "Delicious."

"I helped peel the apples."

"I thought so. They seem especially well peeled this year." Mama smiled and patted the bed beside her. "Would you mind keeping me company for a while?"

Sylvia wasn't sure that Father would approve, but she nodded and climbed into bed, careful not to jostle the tray. She snuggled close and rested her hand on her mama's tummy, waiting for the baby to respond. When an especially strong kick pushed Sylvia's hand away, Mama laughed. "I think he knows his big sister is waiting for him to come out and play."

"Do you really think it's a boy?" asked Sylvia. "Claudia wants another sister." A better sister, Claudia had implied.

"I think so, but we won't know until the day comes." Her mother grimaced and rubbed her lower back. "Which I hope will be soon."

"Not too soon," said Sylvia, thinking of how often she saw her father bent over his calendar in the library, counting and re-counting the weeks as if his diligence could keep the baby from coming.

"No, not too soon," her mother agreed. She finished her breakfast and asked Sylvia to take the tray away so she could lie down again. Sylvia returned the tray to the night-stand and climbed back into bed beside her mother.

Her mother stroked her hair gently. "I've missed you, darling. I'm sorry I haven't been able to play with you."

"That's all right," said Sylvia. "I under-stand."

"After the baby comes, I'll be as right as rain again. You'll see."

Sylvia nodded and hugged her. She wanted to believe it, but the house was so full of apprehension that some days she thought the windows might shatter and the darkness stream from the house like billowing black smoke.

"Everything will be fine, darling," her mother said. "Don't worry."

"I can't help it," Sylvia blurted. "Everyone says not to upset you and I'm trying, I'm really trying, but what if it's already too late? What if the bad luck is already hurting the baby? You touched the quilt, and maybe that's all it takes."

She regretted the words the moment they passed her lips, but to her surprise, her mother let out a gentle laugh. "Oh, Sylvia, is that what's troubling you? That silly superstition?"

That wasn't it. At least, that wasn't everything, but she couldn't bring herself to query her mother about the doctor's visits and Father's constant anxious frowns and the adults' hushed conversations when they did not know children were listening. Sylvia could not give voice to those other fears, so she nodded. Everything would be so much better if only the quilt worried her.

"I promise you that the quilt is not bad luck," her mother said firmly. "How could anything made with so much love bring the baby anything but comfort and happiness?"

"Grandma says the pattern —"

"I know what Grandma says. I've heard the old wives' tales. Have you? Have you really listened to what the folklore says about that pattern?"

"It says —" Sylvia hesitated, trying to remember Grandma's exact words, certain it was a trick question. "If you give a boy a Wandering Foot quilt, he'll be too restless to stay in one place. He'll roam the world, never settling down."

"That's what it says," her mother confirmed. "And although I don't believe the superstition, not for a moment, if that's our little baby's fate, I don't think that's so terrible."

Sylvia propped herself up on her elbows. "You don't?"

"Not at all. What's wrong with a little wanderlust? I like to think that your little brother or sister might have adventures, see the world, and visit all the places I've only read about in books." Her mother reached up and stroked her cheek. "You see, darling, I was always too ill to travel when I was a little girl. My parents took my older sister with them when they went abroad, but I stayed at home in New York with my nanny.

Until I married your father and came to Elm Creek Manor, the most exotic place I had ever visited was our summer house."

"That's not fair. If you couldn't go, they all should have stayed home."

"I admit there were times when I was jealous of my sister, but as I grew older, I resolved to be happy for her. I decided it wouldn't be fair to deny her travel and fun just because I was too fragile to do anything — or so everyone thought." A brief frown clouded her features. "Everyone but my nanny. Now that my sister is gone, I'm grateful that she had so many wonderful experiences when she was young."

Sylvia had to admit that it didn't sound so bad to wander the world and have adventures, not the way her mother put it, but one nagging worry remained. "But what about that part that says he'll never be happy to stay in one place?" she asked. "Doesn't that mean that he won't want to stay here at Elm Creek Manor with the rest of the family? What if he goes far away and we'll never see him again, just like Elizabeth?"

"We don't know that we'll never see Elizabeth again," her mother corrected. "It's a long way to travel, but I'm sure she and Henry will make the journey someday."

Sylvia would be perfectly content if Henry decided to stay behind in California. "But what about the baby?" she persisted. "Either he'll leave Elm Creek Manor, or he'll stay here but be unhappy."

"Well . . ." Mama took a deep breath, sighed, and fell silent for a moment. "Well, babies can't go anywhere on their own, so we have years before that will be a concern. Even after that, perhaps he'll travel a lot, but always come home to the family." She gave herself a little shake. "Why are we even going on like this? It's a silly superstition, nothing we need to fear, and it isn't right to be so gloomy on Christmas morning. The New Year is going to bring us a new baby, and that's cause for joy, not worry."

She tickled Sylvia under her chin until Sylvia giggled, and she resolved, as her mother had so many years ago, to be happy for her little sibling, to think only of the good the superstition might visit upon the family, and not worry about dire predictions that probably would not come to pass. The very idea that any Bergstrom would not be happy at Elm Creek Manor was laughable. Perhaps her little brother would see the world, but surely he would always come home to them. The lucky colors she had stitched into the quilt would see to that.

That quiet Christmas passed and the New Year drew closer. When Mama's condition did not worsen, warm rays of hope began to illuminate the manor. When the subject of New Year's Eve came up around the dinner table, Great-Aunt Lucinda remarked that it would be a shame not to welcome in a year that was sure to be brighter than the one before, a year that was certain to bring the family much happiness. To Sylvia's delight, her father and the other adults of the family agreed.

A Sylvester Ball was out of the question, of course; the family had not celebrated with *Bleigiessen* since the New Year's Eve the leaden shapes foretold Claudia's heart-break and Mama's death. Even though the predictions had not come true, no one could laugh at how they had been frightened and misled. By unspoken agreement, the family had decided not to peer into the future in that way again. The consequences of what they might discover could not be reduced to the triviality of a party game.

Finally they settled for a quiet family observance at home, with a supper of pork crown roast with apples, creamed potatoes with peas, and sauerkraut. Father would make his *Feuerzangenbowle* punch for the adults, Great-Aunt Lucinda would make

Pfannkuchen for everyone, and the girls would be allowed to stay up until midnight to welcome the New Year with noisemakers and apple cider toasts.

Sylvia was so pleased by the idea of a family party that she eagerly offered to help prepare the meal. "She only wants to dip her fingers in the jelly when Great-Aunt Lucinda isn't looking," said Claudia, which made the aunts laugh and Sylvia smolder. Grandma must have believed that Sylvia's offer was sincere, however, for she tutted sympathetically and said that Sylvia could be her special helper.

As they went down to the cellar to retrieve a crock of sauerkraut Great-Aunt Lucinda had made the summer before, Grandma reminded her that the family recipe had been handed down through the years from Gerda Bergstrom, Grandpa's aunt and the finest cook in the Bergstrom family. "I didn't take to the dish at first," she confessed, her voice echoing off the cool, dark walls of the cellar. "The flavor was so sharp and pungent I thought Aunt Gerda had served it to me as a prank. I had to force myself to choke it down, but what else could I do? I was a new bride and I wanted to make a good impression."

"Didn't your mother make sauerkraut?"

"No, but we had our own traditional dishes that might have caught the Bergstrom family by surprise." She smiled to herself and added, "I'd love to see what Lucinda would do if I set a plate of haggis before her."

Sylvia didn't like the sound of any dish that Great-Aunt Lucinda might refuse. "But didn't you eat pork and sauerkraut for the New Year?" Grandma fussed about good luck and bad more than anyone Sylvia knew. It was difficult to imagine that she would knowingly pass up an easy way to bring good luck to the household.

"That's a German tradition. My mother was a Scotswoman, which means that you're part Scot, too." Grandma gestured for Sylvia to help her lift the crock from its low shelf. "My father was Welsh, so you have some of that, as well. You're part English, from your mother's people, and there's a little Swedish on your great-grandfather's side. You're quite a little American mix, aren't you? It's a wonder you're not constantly at war with yourself."

Sylvia had never really thought about it. She was a part of the Bergstrom family, and that was all that mattered.

They carried the crock upstairs to the kitchen. There Grandma instructed Sylvia to put on her apron and help her peel potatoes. Grandma looked thoughtful as she took a potato from the burlap sack on the floor and inspected it for bad spots. "My mother called the celebration of the New Year 'Hogmanay,' " she said, setting the sharp blade of her paring knife against the dusky potato skin.

"What does that mean?" asked Sylvia. By the sound of it, it had something to do with pork, lots of it.

Grandma shrugged. "She never said. I'm not sure she knew. She had so many funny words for ordinary things that I never questioned it." She smiled as she sent potato peelings flying neatly into the trash bin. "I remember we had to clean the house thoroughly before we could give any thought to a celebration. Before midnight on New Year's Eve, the fireplaces had to be swept clean and the ashes carried outside. All debts had to be paid, too. Sometimes my mother would send one of my brothers running to a neighbor's house after supper with a coin or two to pay off a debt, even though most of our neighbors weren't Scottish and wouldn't mind if she waited another day. The purpose was to prepare yourselves and your home to begin the New Year with a fresh, clean slate, with all the problems, mistakes, and strife of the old year forgotten."

"I like that idea," said Sylvia. Her family never seemed to forget any of her mistakes. It would have been nice if a holiday obligated them to try.

"My parents followed other traditions in their homelands that they didn't carry with them to America." Grandma placed a potato in Sylvia's hands. "You can peel while you listen. That's a good girl."

Sylvia peeled the potato slowly, wary of cutting herself. "What did they do in Scotland that they couldn't do in Pennsylvania?"

"It's not that they couldn't. I suppose they could have, but some traditions are simply more enjoyable when everyone in the town joins in." Grandma smiled, remembering. "My mother told me about a tradition called First Footing, which told that the first person who crossed the threshold after the stroke of midnight would determine the luck of the household for the coming year. The year would be especially prosperous if a tall, dark-haired, handsome man was the first to enter the house on the first day of the New Year."

"Why did it have to be a handsome man?" asked Sylvia, placing her peeled potato in the bowl next to Grandma's and reaching for another. "Why not a pretty lady?"

"If the lady was expecting a child, or if she was a new bride, she was also considered to bring good luck," Grandma said. "A blond man, on the other hand, was believed to bring bad luck. My mother said that was because a dark-haired man was assumed to be a fellow Scot, but a blond could be a Viking, come to pillage and plunder. Naturally, since everyone wanted good luck and no one could stay shut up in their homes until the appropriate person came to the door, the tradition changed. Tall, dark-haired, handsome men would be enlisted to go around to the homes of their neighbors, bringing with them symbolic gifts such as coal for the fire, or salt, or a treat like fruit buns or shortbread. No one was supposed to speak to the First Footer until he entered the house, gave them the traditional gifts, and spoke a blessing: 'A good New Year to one and all and many more may you see.' After that you could speak to the guest and offer him a drink of whiskey before he departed for the next house."

"My father would be a good First Footer," said Sylvia. "He's tall, he has dark hair like mine, and he's very handsome. Everyone would be glad to see him on New Year's Eve."

Grandma laughed. "I've always thought he was very handsome, too, but he's my son, so I can't pretend to be impartial. Oh, there's something else my mother told me about that I've always wished I could see. The young men of her village would build large balls about a yard wide from chicken wire, paper, tar, and other materials that would burn. They would attach a chain, light the ball on fire, and walk through the streets of the town swinging the burning fireball around and around. It must have been a dazzling sight, all the young men out in the streets lighting up the darkness with those crackling circles of fire. When the fireballs were almost burned out, or when the young men tired of the game and wanted to celebrate with more whiskey, they would parade down to the riverside and send the fireballs sailing through the air into the water below."

Sylvia shivered with delight. It sounded terribly beautiful, and terribly dangerous. "I probably wouldn't be allowed to try that here," she said.

"Absolutely not," said Grandma. "It's a wonder those Scottish villages weren't burned to the ground, or the young men seriously injured. As much as I'd like just once to see those fireballs swinging, I suppose it's just as well that my mother's family left that tradition behind when they came to America."

"Maybe someday we can go to Scotland for the New Year and see them."

Grandma smiled at her affectionately for a moment before taking up her paring knife again. "Perhaps you will someday, my dear. I hope you travel far and wide and see many beautiful and wondrous things in your lifetime."

Sylvia bit back the impertinent question that immediately sprang to mind: Then why did Grandma fear the Wandering Foot quilt pattern so much? Wasn't what Grandma wished for her exactly what the quilt was supposed to bring?

She almost, but not quite, wished that someone had given her a Wandering Foot quilt when she was a baby. Maybe Claudia's choice wasn't so bad after all — not that Sylvia would ever tell her sister that.

Since Claudia had taken Mama her breakfast tray, Sylvia was granted the honor of serving her the special New Year's Eve dinner. Sylvia entertained her mother by retelling Grandma's stories of Scottish New Year's celebrations and imagining what would happen if she tried to make a fireball of her own. "Your father would have a fit, that's what would happen," her mother said, smiling. "Grandma would never tell you another story out of fear that you might decide to try it."

"How did you celebrate New Year's Eve when you were a little girl, Mama?"

Her mother regarded her with mild surprise, and Sylvia felt a quick flush of shame. It was true that she rarely asked her mother to share stories of her girlhood in New York. Unlike Claudia, she had little interest in descriptions of pretty dresses and fancy balls, of dance lessons and learning good manners. Her mother never spoke of mischief or play, but only of rules and restrictions. Grandfather and Grandmother Lockwood had raised her to be a proper young lady, and since this was the very sort of well-behaved child Sylvia invariably failed to emulate, her mother's stories seemed like dull morality tales. Sylvia had decided long ago that the Bergstrom family was far more interesting than the Lockwoods. Unlike Claudia, who hung on their mother's every word, Sylvia paid little attention when a distant look came into her mother's eyes as she remembered events long ago and far away.

"I really want to know," Sylvia persisted.

"We didn't eat pork and sauerkraut," said

Mama. "My father believed hard work brought one good luck, and my mother put her faith in knowing the right people. My parents almost always went to a New Year's Eve ball at one of their friends' homes or somewhere else in the city. When we were older, my sister and I were allowed to go with them. The men wore elegant coats and tails, and the ladies dressed in stunning gowns and wore their finest jewelry. The orchestra played, we danced and danced, and at midnight we threw streamers and drank champagne. My sister and I were quite grown up by that time," she hastened to add.

"That sounds like fun," Sylvia said gamely.

Mama tried to hide a smile. "You might truly think so when you're older. My favorite New Year's Eve came years before I was allowed to go to fancy balls. I was ten years old in 1900, and the city was electric with anticipation for the turning of the century. My parents and sister celebrated by going to the theater and then to a party at the home of my father's biggest business rival. The men didn't get along, but they ran in the same social circle so they had to include each other in their gatherings or people would talk. They were both glad, too, for any opportunity to show off their wealth and success to the other. If my parents refused the Drurys' invitation, it would be seen as admitting they could not compete or, worse yet, rudeness."

"Your sister got to go but you didn't?" Sylvia exclaimed. "Again?"

"I was too young, and my mother thought I would catch a terrible chill if I stayed out so late on a winter's night."

"That's silly. You would have been indoors almost the whole time. You could have worn a coat."

"That's what I told them. My father and sister stuck up for me, but my mother wouldn't hear of it." Mama smiled and lifted her shoulders as if to say it had happened so long ago that it no longer mattered. "I was terribly disappointed to be left behind. After they left, I went upstairs to work on my Crazy Quilt. It was nearly finished, and stitching upon it usually lifted my spirits, but not that night. A new century was about to begin, and I would have to watch its arrival through a nursery window."

Sylvia stung from the unfairness of it all. "I would have snuck out of the house and followed them."

"The last time I had tried anything like that, I got my nanny fired," said her mother. "I loved her dearly, too, so it was a great loss to me. But after they sent her away, there was no worse punishment they could deliver, or so I thought at the time. I waited for my mother's maid to fall asleep, then I dressed in my warmest clothes and left the house."

Sylvia stared, disbelieving. "Where did you go? What did you do?"

"I walked through the city, enjoying the lights and the celebration. I had a little pocket money, so I bought myself a cup of hot chocolate and a cinnamon doughnut at a small café that my mother would never have considered worthy of her patronage. I walked a long, long time until I came to City Hall Park in lower Manhattan. I had overheard other passersby say that there would be fireworks at midnight, and I thought there could be no better way to welcome the New Year than with fireworks.

"I had never seen such a crowd, and I was thrilled to be a part of it. Everywhere, people were laughing and singing, too distracted with their own fun to notice one little girl all alone. Finally, at the stroke of midnight, City Hall went dark for just a moment, and then suddenly all the lights came on and fireworks lit up the sky. All around me people were cheering and kissing, and sometimes, above the din, I heard the bells of Trinity Church ringing in the New Year several blocks away.

"Then, suddenly, I felt a hand on my shoulder. 'Miss Lockwood?' I heard a man ask. He spun me around and I found myself looking up into an unfamiliar face, rough and incredulous.

"I gulped and spoke not a word. 'You're the younger Miss Lockwood, aren't you?' the man asked. I didn't see any point in denying it, so I nodded. He glanced around for my parents, but of course, they were nowhere to be found. 'What are you doing out here all alone?' he asked. 'This is no place for a girl like you.'

"When I offered no explanation, he shook his head and said that I must return home at once. He told me he worked on the loading docks at my father's store, and he had seen me come in just days before to pick out my Christmas present, as my sister and I were allowed to do every year. He took me firmly by the shoulder and steered me out of the crowd. Somehow he managed to hail a cab, and he gave the driver strict instructions to take me home and not to leave until he saw me safely inside. I was mortified when the man dug into his pockets and counted out change to pay my fare. I knew he couldn't possibly earn very much;

the low wages of my father's store employees had been a constant source of disagreement between him and my nanny, who supported workers' rights to form unions. I wanted to apologize, but I was speechless from embarrassment. I could only nod as he warned me never to do such a dangerous thing again, shut the cab door, and waved the driver on."

"You were so naughty," breathed Sylvia.

"Oh, don't I know it, but I was lucky, too. I crept off to bed and was sound asleep long before my parents and sister returned home."

"Did they ever find out?"

"At first, I wasn't sure." Mama finished her supper, wiped her lips, and set the tray on the nightstand. "My father stayed home from work on New Year's Day, but he kept to himself in his study and I only saw him at mealtimes. I watched my mother carefully to see if she suspected anything, but she was too busy going over every detail of the previous night's party with her maid, Harriet. My sister assured me that the play had been dull and the party afterward even worse, but I knew she was only saying so to make me think I had not missed out on anything. I didn't breathe a word of my New Year's Eve adventure even to her, and

I was relieved that I had apparently gotten away with it.

"The next day my father returned to work and, as usual, did not come home until supper late that evening. My mother, sister, and I were already seated when he strode in and took his place at the head of the table. 'Did you hear about the panic at City Hall Park two nights ago?' he asked us.

" 'Of course, my dear,' my mother told him. 'I do read the papers, you know. It was all over the *Times*. Some of the worst of it happened right in front of its building.'

"I kept silent while my sister begged our father to explain. I then learned that I had unwittingly been part of a historically momentous gathering. Remember that I told you I heard the bells of Trinity Church from where I stood at City Hall Park, several blocks away? An enormous crowd had massed in the narrow strip around the church, as well, and as the night went on, both gatherings swelled to such numbers that the two crowds, thousands strong, merged on Broadway. The revelers made merry until shortly after midnight, but then chaos erupted as people set off at cross-purposes, some trying to make it to the Brooklyn Bridge, others fighting their way uptown. Families were separated, and a child was trampled underfoot as the revelers pushed against one another. It was a terrifying scene, and the police could do little to manage it.

"I had been sent home in my cab only moments before the panic started. I gaped at my father, thinking of what a narrow escape I'd had. 'Was anyone hurt?' my sister asked.

" 'One child was injured,' my father said, 'but it could have been much worse. Thankfully both of my little girls were safely far away from that midnight disaster.' And with that he raised his eyebrows at me as if daring me to disagree."

"The man from the store tattled on you," said Sylvia.

"He probably thought it was his duty to tell his employer that his little girl had put herself in great danger," said Mama. "I don't find any fault with him. That little child who was trampled could have been me. I didn't have any grown-ups around to hold my hand or pull me out of harm's way. If I had not left City Hall Park when I did, my New Year might have had a tragic beginning."

"I can't believe you left the house alone at night," marveled Sylvia. "Did your father spank you? Did he tell your mother?"

"Goodness, no. If he had, I'm sure she

would have locked me in my room for a week. I received no punishment for what I had done, and in fact, my father never spoke of it again." Mother smiled, her gaze distant. "It was the most adventurous, most disobedient thing I had ever done, and would ever do, until I married your father."

"Why was marrying Father disobedient?" said Sylvia. "Didn't your parents like him?"

Her mother hesitated as if regretting the mention. "Oh, I suppose they liked him well enough, but they wanted me to marry someone else. I wanted to please them, but I loved your father, so I married him instead."

Sylvia shook her head at this new, unbelievable revelation. As difficult as it was to imagine her mother as a naughty little girl, it was impossible to believe that anyone would want Mama to marry someone other than Father. Sylvia couldn't imagine either of them loving anyone else.

"After making such a disobedient start to a new century, I resolved never again to defy my parents out of anger or jealousy," said Mama. "The New Year wasn't only a time for celebration, you see. It was also a time for reflection, and for deciding to mend one's ways and change one's life for the better." Sylvia's mother put her arms around her and kissed her on the top of the head. "You could do that, you know. Think about how you would like to improve yourself in the year ahead and make a New Year's resolution to change."

Sylvia frowned, thinking. "I'd like to run faster," she announced. "I think I'll resolve to do that."

Her mother laughed. "Very well. Deciding how to improve yourself is the first step. Now, how would you go about achieving that goal?"

"Practice? Maybe if I try to run a little faster each day, by next year I'll be lots faster."

"That sounds like the right way to do it. But practice only outside or in the nursery," Mama hastened to add. "I don't think Grandma and the aunts would like to see you running through the halls. For your first New Year's resolution, I think that's fine, but you should know that most resolutions are meant to improve one's character rather than one's athletic skills."

"You mean like . . . not fighting with your sister?"

"Exactly," said Mama. "In fact, that's a resolution most people in this house would be very happy to see you keep."

Sylvia hadn't meant that resolution for

herself, but for Claudia. Still, she supposed she could keep it, too, and better than her big sister could.

Father appeared in the doorway then, so Sylvia carried her mother's dishes to the kitchen and ran off to play, thinking of New Year's resolutions and her mother's New Year's Eve adventure so long ago. If Sylvia had been in her mother's place, she would have resolved to have more exciting escapades like that one, instead of promising to be less defiant. It sounded like her mother had only been defiant that one night, so why should she have to resolve to change? It must have been unbearable to stay behind so often and watch her sister go out into the city with their parents. Grandmother and Grandfather Lockwood should have made resolutions to treat their daughters more fairly. Certain members of the Bergstrom family ought to do the same.

In fact, Sylvia thought as she climbed the stairs to the nursery where she kept paper and pencil, everyone in the family would benefit from making New Year's resolutions, and she knew exactly which ones were most necessary.

Sylvia wrote, crossed out mistakes, and copied her writing over neatly on fresh sheets of paper as night fell. She rolled the pages into fancy scrolls and tied them with ribbons, and she had just hidden them in her sewing basket when Claudia came upstairs and summoned her down to the ballroom. Great-Aunt Lucinda had set out *Pfannkuchen* and apple cider, and everyone was gathering for the New Year's Eve party. Father had spent all evening by Mama's side, looking through photo albums and reading aloud, but when Mama wanted to sleep, he joined the rest of the family downstairs by the fire. The adults of the family told jokes and stories of New Year's Eves past, remembering loved ones that Sylvia knew only through family legends. Great-Grandfather Hans and Great-Grandmother Anneke, who had come to America from Germany and founded Elm Creek Farm. Hans's sister, Gerda, who never married but had loved to read and discuss politics and cook. Sylvia drifted off to sleep to the murmur of their voices, but Grandma gently shook her awake five minutes before midnight so she could count down the last seconds of the old year with everyone else. When the mantel clock chimed midnight, she jumped up and down, blew on her tin horn, and shouted, "Happy New Year!" louder than anyone, but after that, she did not argue when her father sent her upstairs to bed.

First, though, she wanted to wish her mother Happy New Year. A light shone through the crack beneath her mother's bedroom door, so Sylvia knocked and softly called out to her. When she did not reply, Sylvia slowly pushed open the door and found her mother sleeping soundly, her book resting open on the bed.

Sylvia tiptoed across the room, bent over to kiss her mother's thin cheek, and picked up the book so her mother wouldn't roll on top of it while she slept. The envelope with the New York postmark Mama had been using as a bookmark lay on the nightstand, but the flap had been opened since Sylvia had last seen it.

She glanced at her sleeping mother, then back to the doorway where she expected her father to appear any moment, then set the book facedown on the bed and quickly slipped a single, thick page from the envelope. When she unfolded it, a newspaper clipping fluttered to the floor. Sylvia quickly scooped it up; a quick glance revealed a society page story about a Christmas ball in New York that the elegantly dressed couple in the photograph had apparently hosted. Sylvia didn't recognize the faces in the photograph or any of the names, so she turned her attention to the letter.

The message, written in firm, dark strokes on ivory writing paper edged in black, began abruptly: "Mrs. Edwin Corville enjoys every luxury, while you waste yourself on a horse farmer in the middle of godforsaken nowhere. Your wishes for a Happy New Year ring hollow, as does the news of your condition. How a strong-willed young woman like yourself can submit to the demands of a husband who clearly has no regard for the risks to your health never ceases to astonish me."

Sylvia swallowed hard and returned the letter and the clipping to the envelope, tucked them into the book, and set it on the nightstand. Mama would think Father had moved them; she would never know Sylvia had read Grandmother Lockwood's cruel words. A sudden thought struck Sylvia: Did Father know what Mama's mother thought of him? Mama had said her parents had wanted her to marry another man, and it seemed Grandmother Lockwood had never forgiven her.

Sylvia bit her lips together, turned off the lamp, and hurried from the room. She climbed into bed, sick at heart. This couldn't be the first ugly letter Grandmother Lockwood had sent, or Mama would have shown some sign of shock or remorse. All the other letters, all of Mama's stories, must have been edited for a little girl's ears. Was Mama a liar? It was unthinkable. Was she ashamed?

Sylvia drifted off to a troubled sleep.

The next morning she woke late, the letter a vague and unpleasant memory fading like a dream. She hurried downstairs just in time to stop Grandma before she set the kitchen table for breakfast. "It's a holiday. Why don't we eat in the dining room?" she asked. "I'll set the table."

Grandma blinked with surprise at her breathless suggestion, in part, perhaps, because Sylvia rarely agreed to a chore without arguing that Claudia ought to help, too. "I suppose that's fine," she said, waving Sylvia off to the task. "Use the good dishes."

Sylvia did, but not before racing up two flights to the nursery and stuffing her pockets with the ribbon-tied scrolls she had prepared the night before. Sylvia tucked one beside each plate and finished setting the table just as Great-Aunt Lydia came in carrying a platter of hot sausages. "What's this?" she asked, smiling at the sight of the scrolls. "It seems we're having a rather formal breakfast this morning, complete with place cards."

"It's a New Year's surprise," said Sylvia, fairly bouncing with excitement. She hurried off to the kitchen to help carry plates to the table. Claudia had taken a tray up to their mother, but she came down right away, disappointed, and reported that Mama was sleeping. Claudia had covered the dishes and left the tray on the nightstand.

Sylvia's thoughts flew to the book, and the letter tucked inside. She studied Claudia's face, but her expression betrayed no shock or alarm, only disappointment that she had not been able to eat New Year's Day breakfast with their mother. Claudia had not read the letter, Sylvia decided, and that was no surprise, for Claudia would never dream of sneaking glances at her mother's private letters. Sylvia wished she had been as good a daughter the night before.

Claudia took her seat as Grandma and Great-Aunt Lucinda began to pass around serving dishes piled high with scrambled eggs, juicy sausages, potatoes fried with onions and peppers, and *Pfannkuchen* left over from the night before. "What's this thing?" Claudia asked, picking up the scroll Sylvia had tucked beneath the edge of her plate.

"It's Sylvia's New Year's Day surprise,"

135

said Great-Aunt Lydia.

Great-Aunt Lucinda fingered her scroll warily. "I'm almost afraid to open it."

"Go ahead." Sylvia took a *Pfannkuchen* from the platter and set it on her plate, licking the sugar from her fingertips. "It's not scary."

"Napkin, Sylvia," her father said, untying his own scroll.

No one spoke as they read the words Sylvia had written for each of them. Sylvia ate her breakfast and looked around the table, watching their faces expectantly. With a start, she remembered that she had forgotten to make a scroll for her mother. That's all right, she decided. Mama was perfect exactly as she was.

Suddenly Claudia shrilled, "Is this supposed to be funny?"

Great-Aunt Lucinda laughed. "Mine certainly is. 'One: Bake more cookies. Two: Not just at Christmas. Three: Let Sylvia have as many turns to take the breakfast tray up to Mama as Claudia gets.' She ran out of space or I suppose I'd have more suggestions."

"I only have one," said Great-Aunt Lydia. "I must not need as much improvement as you, sister."

"Mine will be a little difficult to fulfill,"

said Grandma wistfully. " 'Go to Scotland to watch the swinging fireballs.' "

"The swinging what?" asked Great-Aunt Lucinda.

"That's between me and my granddaughter." Grandma rolled up her scroll, slipped the ribbon around it, and gave Sylvia a little wink.

Sylvia's father was shaking his head, his mouth twisted wryly. " 'Let Mama do whatever she wants.' Sylvia, if you think I could do otherwise, you haven't been paying attention."

"Why are you laughing?" Claudia cried. "This isn't funny!"

All the adults turned to her in surprise. "Why, Claudia, what does your scroll say?" asked Grandma.

"This ought to be good," said Great-Aunt Lucinda.

"I'm not going to read it," said Claudia. "It's mean."

"No, it isn't," protested Sylvia. "It's a resolution."

"It could still be mean," said Father, a mild note of warning in his voice. "Go ahead, Claudia. Tell us what it says."

Her eyes red, her jaw set, Claudia took a deep breath and reluctantly read her scroll aloud. " 'One: Stop being so bossy. Two:

Stop hogging Mama. Three: Stop hogging everything. Four: Be nice to Sylvia.' I am nice to you, you little brat. A lot nicer than you deserve." She flung down the scroll and folded her arms. "I'm not going to read any more of these insults."

"They're not insults; they're New Year's resolutions," Sylvia explained. "They're promises you make so you can improve yourself."

"I know what a resolution is," snapped Claudia. "You're not supposed to make them for other people. You're supposed to make them for yourself."

"I did make one for myself," said Sylvia, taking the last scroll from her pocket.

Great-Aunt Lucinda's eyebrows shot up. "And what does that say?"

" 'Don't fight with your sister.' "

The adults burst into laughter. Sylvia looked around the table in puzzlement. Grandma wiped tears from her eyes; Father snorted into his handkerchief; Claudia seethed and glared. Sylvia felt like she was choking. No one had ever explicitly told her that she was supposed to make resolutions for herself alone, but now it seemed so obvious she did not know how she could have misunderstood. Of course it was rude to tell other people what they were doing wrong

138

and how to change; it was especially rude for a child to say so to an adult. What would be worse: allowing the family to believe she was a thoughtless little girl, or to reveal the truth, that she was too stupid to know how New Year's resolutions were supposed to be made?

She decided she would rather be thought rude than ignorant, so she shrugged, stared fiercely at her plate, and willed the tears away. "I was only trying to help."

"Some help you are," snapped Claudia, shoving back her chair. "You've already broken your own New Year's resolution, and it isn't even nine o'clock!"

Miserable, Sylvia sank down in her chair as Claudia marched from the room, probably on her way up to Mama's bedroom to tell her what Sylvia had done. Sylvia wished she could run after her sister and beg her to stop, but Claudia would assume Sylvia's only concern was to avoid their mother's disapproval. Claudia didn't know about that letter from Grandmother Lockwood, and how sad their mother certainly was, no matter how well she hid it. Now Sylvia had made everything worse. The doctor said unpleasant news was not good for Mama and the baby, and because of Sylvia's thoughtlessness, Mama would wake to learn that her daughters had already spoiled the bright, fresh new start of the New Year.

From the corner of her eye, Sylvia saw her father shaking his head in exasperation, while Great-Aunt Lucinda rested her chin on her hand, ruefully watching the doorway through which Claudia had departed. Great-Aunt Lydia sighed and stirred sugar into her coffee, as if that would rid the morning of its bitter taste. Only Grandma did not seem concerned. Her eyes had a faraway look, as if she were imagining blazing fireballs swinging in brilliant arcs against a starry night sky.

Nine days later, Sylvia's mother gave birth to a robust, cheerful little boy. In the excitement and joy that surrounded his arrival, everyone forgot about Sylvia's ribbon-tied scrolls — everyone except Claudia, who never forgot a slight. Whenever the girls disagreed about whose turn it was to rock their darling baby brother to sleep or sing him a lullaby, Claudia reminded Sylvia of her resolution not to fight with her. What choice did Sylvia have then but to give in? Claudia kept a running tally of how many times Sylvia broke her resolution until spring, when she lost count as well as interest and found new ways to annoy Sylvia instead.

Although Sylvia had to share baby Richard with Claudia the way she had to share everything, she doted on him. From the start she resolved that she would make up for her mistakes as a little sister by being the loving and protective big sister he deserved. Her resolution would be no less binding for all that it came on January 10 instead of the first day of the year.

Sylvia never mentioned New Year's resolutions in her sister's presence again. In years to come, whenever Sylvia made a resolution for herself, she wrote it on a scroll of paper and tied it with a ribbon as a reminder of that unhappy morning and how she should look to her own faults and failings before trying to correct others'. Every New Year's Eve, she would untie the scroll of the year before and read over the vows she had made. Sometimes she noted with pride how she had kept her resolution and had reaped the rewards of her diligence and self-discipline; more often she looked back ruefully upon her optimism of a year ago, when the hope and promise of the New Year had made high goals seem within reach, and difficult resolutions easier to keep than they would prove to be.

With the excitement of the wedding and their sorrow over Andrew's children's disapproval, Sylvia had been too distracted to give much thought to New Year's resolutions that season. She had a few she wished Andrew's children would make, but as she had learned all too well that New Year's morning so long ago, she could not make those decisions for anyone but herself. If she ever forgot, the New Year's Reflections quilt would remind her, for she had sewn the lessons learned into the quilt. A Wandering Foot block called to mind the dangers of blindly fearing superstition, for what one person shunned as misfortune could be welcomed as a blessing by someone else. A Year's Favorite pattern honored her brother's birth, reminding her of her mother's patience and endurance, and the great happiness that was her reward. And the Resolution Square block reminded her that she could wish for positive change in another person, she could even lovingly nurture it, but ultimately, she could control no one's behavior but her own, and often that was where the real problem resided.

As the taxi pulled up in front of the theater, Sylvia imagined her mother as a little girl boldly stepping out into a festive night, welcoming the turn of the century with curiosity and excitement. She thought of her Grandma, entranced by her own mother's stories of the New Year in a faraway land, longing to see those wonders for herself but never venturing forth, so she had only her mother's stories and no memories of her own to pass down to her granddaughter. What would those two beloved women think of the turns Sylvia's life had taken, of the resolutions made and broken, of the adventures she had gladly embarked upon and those she had been drawn into unwillingly?

Andrew paid the driver and helped Sylvia from the taxi. "You were lost in thought the whole drive over," he said, escorting her into the warmth of the theater lobby. "Adele's story was amazing, wasn't it? It's funny to think what can come of a simple New Year's resolution."

Sylvia was too ashamed of her childhood foolishness to explain the real reason for her reverie. "Adele made the right resolution at the right time for the right person," she replied instead, "and that made all the difference."

CHAPTER THREE

The next morning, Sylvia and Andrew woke beneath Adele's antique quilt in the elegant four-poster bed in the Garden Room, well rested and refreshed despite their late night at the theater. After the show, they had wandered along Broadway arm in arm, stopping for dessert and coffee at My Most Favorite Dessert Company. "We can't go wrong at a place with a name like that," Andrew said, opening the door for Sylvia with a flourish.

He turned out to be right. The three-layer chocolate ganache cake Sylvia enjoyed was so rich and heavenly that she swore she wouldn't be able to eat a bite for breakfast, but in the morning, delicious aromas from Adele's kitchen beckoned her from Andrew's arms. She kissed him good morning, then folded back the beautiful quilt, gave it an affectionate pat, and hurried off to the shower. They had a full day planned, and

Sylvia could not wait to begin.

The other guests were just sitting down at the table when Sylvia and Andrew arrived. As Adele and Julius served the meal, everyone introduced themselves and chatted about their excursions in New York. Most were holiday vacationers, some from overseas; Sylvia was pleased to learn that one of the couples, Karl and Erika, resided in a small village not far from Baden-Baden, Germany, the ancestral home of the Bergstrom family. "You must tell me all about it," Sylvia exclaimed, delighted.

"Have you never visited?" asked Karl.

Sylvia was embarrassed to admit that she never had. She had always meant to, but as the years passed, it had seemed increasingly unlikely that she ever would. Erika promised to act as Sylvia's own personal tour guide if she ever did make the journey, and in the meantime, she would be happy to show Sylvia the pictures of her hometown stored on her digital camera.

One couple from upstate was in town visiting relatives who did not have room in their cramped apartment for extended family. "I'd rather stay here anyway," the woman confided. "My daughter-in-law couldn't make a breakfast this tasty with four cookbooks and two days to prepare, and I know, because she's tried."

Sylvia smiled politely as the other guests chuckled, resisting the urge to point out that the woman was fortunate her daughter-in-law was willing to go to so much trouble for someone who clearly would not appreciate her efforts. One cookbook and a couple of hours was all Sylvia had ever been willing to put into a meal. But Sylvia held her tongue, unwilling to ruin the friendly mood around the table. She knew, too, that the woman had only meant to compliment their hostess — and that she herself was too easily provoked of late by any show of disapproval between in-laws.

The conversation turned to the holiday season and the upcoming New Year. Sylvia told Karl and Erika about the German traditions her family had celebrated in America — eating pork and sauerkraut to bring good luck, enjoying delicious sweets like *Pfannkuchen,* indulging in the rum punch made over the fire, and trying to glimpse the future by interpreting lead shapes in a bowl of water.

"Not so many people make *Feuerzangenbowle* anymore," said Karl with regret. "It is so much easier to open a beer."

"My uncles still make it every New Year's Eve," said Erika. "But lead pouring is out of favor. No one wants their children playing with lead near the fire, breathing in those toxic fumes! Nowadays, one uses melted candle wax, and I suppose the predictions are no more or no less accurate than they used to be."

Sylvia smiled, but her heart sank a little. She knew it was foolish, but she had always imagined the place of Great-Grandfather Hans's birth to be frozen in time, exactly as it had been when he departed for America, exactly as the family stories had preserved it. Of course it had grown and changed with the times, just as Elm Creek Manor had.

"We still enjoy the Sylvester Balls," Erika assured her, perhaps sensing her disappointment. "And dinner for one."

"That doesn't sound very festive," said Andrew. "In America, no one wants to spend New Year's Eve alone."

"Nor do we, necessarily," said Karl. "We gather together with family and friends and watch together."

The mother-in-law from upstate looked confused. "Watch what?"

"The television," said Erika. "Or video, if you have other plans and don't want to schedule everything around a broadcast."

Sylvia was utterly lost. "So . . . you eat supper alone, and later you meet to watch television?" She did not want to insult their new German friends, but she thought they would have done better to stick to *Pfann-kuchen, Feuerzangenbowle,* and *Bleigiessen.*

Karl's deep laugh boomed. "No, *Dinner for One,* the television play, of course."

"Of course," echoed Andrew, but his expression of utter bewilderment told Sylvia he was no better enlightened than she.

"It wouldn't be New Year's Eve without it," said Erika. She glanced around the table at the other guests. "Surely you've seen it. It's in English, after all."

"Miss Sophie? James?" Karl added helpfully. "The same procedure as every year?"

His question met with blank stares. Incredulous, the German couple fired off other names — Sir Toby, Admiral von Schneider, Mr. Pommeroy, Mr. Winterbottom — only to learn that their native English-speaking companions did not recognize a single one. "Everyone in Germany watches *Dinner for One* on New Year's Eve," said Karl. "I myself have seen it at least fifty times."

"It's a television skit," Erika explained. "It was written in the 1920s for the British cabaret, but the version we Germans know best was filmed in the early 1960s in front of a live audience in Hamburg. It's been shown on German television every New Year's Eve since the 1970s."

"All the stations broadcast it," said Karl, searching their faces as if he still could not believe they were unaware of the tradition. "It's almost impossible to avoid seeing it on the holiday."

Not that anyone *tried* to avoid it, the German couple added. The comical black-and-white skit was as integral to a German New Year's celebration as they assumed dropping the ball in Times Square was to New Yorkers. The heroine of the story — Karl and Erika broke into fits of laughter as they explained — was Miss Sophie, an elderly British aristocrat celebrating her birthday as she did every year, with a dinner party attended by four dear old friends, blissfully ignoring the unfortunate truth that the men had passed away years ago. Rather than ruin the celebration, Miss Sophie's butler, James, not only serves the meal but also fills in for the absent gentlemen — mimicking their voices, offering birthday toasts, and draining their glasses. As each course begins, James inquires, "The same procedure as last year, Miss Sophie?" to which the lady replies, "The same procedure as every year, James." With each course and round of drinks, James becomes more and more

149

intoxicated — stumbling about, tripping over the tiger skin rug, sending a platter of chicken flying through the air. At the end of the meal, Miss Sophie announces that the party was wonderful, but now she wishes to retire. James links his arm through hers and repeats the now-familiar refrain: "The same procedure as last year, Miss Sophie?" Miss Sophie answers, "The same procedure as *every* year, James." James steadies himself on the staircase banister, declares "Well, I'll do my very best," and gives the unseen studio audience a broad wink before escorting Miss Sophie upstairs.

Sylvia found herself smiling, not because the broad slapstick sounded particularly funny, but because Karl and Erika's inexplicable fondness for the show was amusing to see. "It's a bit ribald at the end, isn't it?" she said.

"I don't get it," said the mother-in-law from upstate.

"I think it's probably one of those shows that gets funnier the more times you watch it," said Andrew, ever the diplomat.

"Absolutely," Erika agreed. "It's funnier with a group of friends, too. Some people watch in bars, and shout out all the lines with the characters. Others watch at home and prepare the same meal James serves

Miss Sophie — Mulligatawny soup, North Sea haddock, chicken, and fruit. Still others use the show to play a drinking game, finishing a beer every time the refrain comes around, or drinking the same liquors James does as he makes each guest's toasts to Miss Sophie."

"I don't recommend that unless you want to start your New Year very, very ill," warned Karl. "Although some say the skit is most humorous when one is as drunk as James."

"Too much imbibing on New Year's Eve is an American tradition, too," said Sylvia. "I never found anything amusing about that, myself." For all that the Bergstroms had enjoyed her father's rum punch, drunkenness had been unacceptable in their family, and it was not something Sylvia tolerated in others, either. She could never have married Andrew if he had been what in their day had been called "a drinking man."

"Where are you going to watch *Dinner for One* this year?" Andrew inquired.

Karl and Erika exchanged a look. "We thought we would watch on the television in our room," said Erika, "but I suppose that won't be possible."

"We assumed everyone in the States watched it, too," said Karl, with a shrug that asked, why wouldn't you?

151

"I don't think that show has ever been broadcast here," said Adele. "I'll look into it and see what I can do."

"We've seen it so often that we can miss it once and still have a happy New Year," said Erika, but she did not sound convinced. "You shouldn't go to any trouble."

"It's no trouble at all," said Adele. "That would be nothing compared to last year, when a Danish family stayed with us. On the morning of December thirty-first, they suddenly absolutely had to have dishes. You know, dinner plates and such. I offered them several from our cupboard, but for some reason those wouldn't do. I assumed they wanted some to take home for souvenirs, so I offered directions to Tiffany's and Bergdorf Goodman. That wasn't what they wanted, either. Finally I directed them to the Arthritis Foundation Thrift Shop at Third and Seventy-Ninth, where they found some old dishes on sale. I had never seen anyone so happy over old dishes, and I thought it was a very odd souvenir, but of course I didn't say anything. Later that night, I learned that in Denmark, it's the custom to throw old dishes at the doors of your friends' homes on New Year's Eve. The more shards of broken dinnerware on your doorstep on January first, the more popular you are. Our Danish guests had been worried that the neighbors would think Julius and I had no friends, so they smashed all those old dishes on our front stoop. It was a mess, but I didn't want to offend them by not respecting their tradition."

"At least they said it was a Danish tradition," Julius broke in. "We wouldn't have known. They might have been playing a New Year's Eve prank on us."

"Maybe practical jokes are the real tradition," said Andrew, and the other guests laughed.

"How do you suppose we'll spend New Year's Eve?" asked Sylvia as she and Andrew returned to the Garden Room after breakfast.

"I'm not sure," said Andrew. "Amy never made a big deal out of the New Year. She loves Christmas, Thanksgiving, Easter, Halloween, Arbor Day —"

"Arbor Day?"

"She likes to plant trees," Andrew explained. "But she never got too excited about New Year's Eve."

Sylvia found it difficult to believe that someone who enjoyed holidays — including the most obscure — would be indifferent to the New Year's celebrations. "What about when Amy and Bob were young? Your family must have kept some New Year's traditions Amy has passed down to her own children."

"Well, sure, we had a few. When Amy and Bob were kids, they could never stay awake long enough to ring in the New Year at the proper time. Katy would set the grandfather clock in the hall ahead so they could hear it strike midnight, and we'd toast the New Year with apple juice at nine o'clock. That routine fell by the wayside as the kids grew up. When Amy was a teenager, she babysat for other families in the neighborhood so the parents could go out and celebrate. She and my wife used to spend New Year's Day watching home movies while Bob and I watched football, but I don't know if you'd call that a tradition. If Amy's ever made a New Year's resolution, she's kept it to herself." Andrew searched his memory for a moment, but then shook his head. "If you're looking for a big celebration, we should stay in New York and watch the ball drop in Times Square. I hope you're not disappointed."

"I won't be disappointed unless Amy leaves us standing on the front porch with our suitcases," Sylvia promised. To her dismay, Andrew snorted as if he considered that a realistic possibility.

Sylvia's thoughts of New Year's celebrations — and fears that she and Andrew might indeed be left outside in the snow upon their arrival in Hartford — soon faded as she and Andrew embarked upon what Sylvia was sure would be the highlight of their stay in New York.

They hailed a cab and drove through the crush of morning traffic toward Fifth Avenue. As they rode along Central Park, snow falling lightly upon the windshield, Sylvia reached for Andrew's hand and held it tightly. She had no idea why she was so nervous. This visit to her mother's childhood home was long overdue, and why she had not at least driven past the old Lockwood house on one of her previous visits to New York, she could not say. It was not a lack of curiosity that had prevented her. Perhaps it was a sense that her mother had not been happy there, and that she would not have wanted to burden Sylvia with her unhappiness.

The cab let them out in front of a stately home facing the park. Sylvia took in the marble façade and the ornate front gate, admiring and yet uncertain. Nothing of the elegant building spoke to her of her mother, although she could not pick out any particular detail that did not fit with her mother's stories.

"Are you ready?" asked Andrew, offering her his arm as she stood rooted on the sidewalk, business people and tourists flowing past her. Sylvia managed a nod and forced herself to approach the front entrance, where Andrew rang the bell.

The woman who answered was dressed in a brilliant rose-colored sari. "You must be Sylvia and Andrew," she said, smiling and beckoning the couple indoors. "I'm Aruna Bhansali. I'm so pleased that you wished to visit. How exciting it is to meet the granddaughter of our home's first resident!"

"Thank you so much for indulging me," said Sylvia. She introduced Andrew as they removed their coats, admiring the elegant foyer. It was warmly lit and inviting, with white marble floors, vases of red calla lilies on a pair of mahogany tables flanking the entrance to a drawing room, and brightly painted carvings of Hindu gods and goddesses displayed in arched nooks. An elegant curved staircase rose gracefully to the second story, and Sylvia imagined her mother as a little girl carefully descending them, her hand raised to grasp the banister.

Aruna showed them to a parlor, where she offered them tea and asked Sylvia to tell her all about her grandparents. Sylvia hated to disappoint her hostess, but she had little information to share. It had never occurred to her that the current owners would be as curious about her family as Sylvia was to see the house where her mother had once lived. To her relief, Aruna seemed pleased with the sparse details Sylvia offered about her grandfather's famous department store, their high-society lives, and Eleanor's decision to leave it all behind to marry a horse farmer from rural Pennsylvania. "How romantic," Aruna said, sighing wistfully. "I always suspected this grand old place had an intriguing history."

"I wish I could tell you more about it," confessed Sylvia. "I couldn't tell you why my grandfather chose that marble, or why he was apparently so fond of classical architectural styles. He was a rather remote figure in my mother's life, I'm afraid, and he figures only very rarely in stories from her childhood."

Aruna smiled. "Perhaps she told you more than you know. You may remember some of those stories as we walk through the house."

Sylvia eagerly finished her tea and followed Aruna as she showed them around the first floor, through rooms that were obviously designed to entertain in high style, to Mr. Bhansali's home office, once a drawing room. The bright colors and Indian décor were nothing the Lockwoods would have chosen for themselves, and yet Sylvia could imagine the successful businessman and society wife at home there.

Upstairs, Aruna showed them bedrooms for family members and household servants, and asked if Sylvia knew which one had been her mother's. Sylvia shook her head. "All I remember is that her nanny had the room next door to hers," she said. "My mother spent most of her time in the nursery."

Aruna brightened and led them up another flight of stairs to a large room with a fireplace, dormer windows, and the smell of incense in the air. Paintings and gold-embroidered silk adorned the walls, and soft rugs and pillows invited the visitors to sit on the floor. It looked nothing like a child's playroom, and yet —

"This must be it," said Sylvia, turning around to take in every detail. How many hours had her mother passed within these walls, playing, dreaming, longing for adventure in the world beyond the front gate? Her mother had called the nursery her refuge, even after she had become a young woman. Had she written letters to her beloved nanny on that window seat? Had she watched from the window, hoping Sylvia's father would appear?

Andrew went to one window and peered outside. "There's a great view of the park."

"That's why I chose this room for my very own," said Aruna. "It's my retreat from the world, the one place in all of New York that feels most like home to me."

"I believe my mother felt very much the same," said Sylvia softly, wishing she could ask her if it was true. When she held quite still, she could imagine her mother's light footsteps on the wooden floor, her quiet laugh, her gentle kiss. When she closed her eyes, she felt her mother standing beside her, welcoming her home.

It had been far too long since Sylvia had felt the warmth of her mother's embrace. What she would not give to have even one of those days back to live again, one of those ordinary days she had taken for granted because it seemed impossible that they would not stretch on endlessly into the future.

Sylvia was ten years old when her mother died. In the years to come, she would wonder if Grandma's death in 1928 and the Great Depression had hastened her mother's decline. Surely the new hardships the family faced worried her, and she was deeply concerned for their less fortunate neighbors. But upon reflection, Sylvia always came to the same conclusion: Her mother had lived far longer than anyone had thought possible, and she had regarded every day as a gift. She loved her family so deeply that she would have clung to life longer to see them through those difficult times, if she could have. In her heart of hearts, Sylvia knew her mother regretted leaving them at a time of such uncertainty.

None of the Bergstroms could bear to celebrate Christmas of 1930, with Mama's death so recent and the wound of their grief so raw. They made their religious observances with heavy hearts and wrapped gifts for Richard, almost four years old, but as December wore on, no one could bear to decorate a tree or bake the famous Bergstrom apple strudel. The old traditions that had once brought them such joy would bring them no comfort that first Christmas without Mama.

The entire season so pained Sylvia that she could not wait for it to end so she could return to school and lose herself in books and math homework. She grieved for her loss, for her own loneliness, but she felt sorrier for Richard than for herself. She had enjoyed nine Merry Christmases with her mother, but Richard had been granted only three, and he would not remember those. Sylvia could not decide if it was a blessing or another great cruelty that he would never realize the dearth that was life in their mother's absence.

To Sylvia's surprise, Santa did not forget any of the Bergstrom children, but left presents for them beneath a small Christmas tree that had miraculously appeared in the ballroom Christmas morning. Richard whooped for joy and played with empty boxes with almost as much delight as with his new ball and toy fire truck, but most of the grown-ups sat quietly, watching the children open their gifts and mustering up smiles when Richard amused them. After the last gift was opened, Father departed swiftly and silently; Great-Aunt Lucinda watched him go, grief etched in the lines of her face, but no one interfered. Sylvia wanted to run after him because wherever he was headed had to be better than the ballroom, where they went through the motions of the holiday when no one felt like celebrating, where the once-festive manor echoed with her mother's absence. The quiet of the snowy woods, the muskiness of the barn, the warmth of the stable — any place would do, anywhere but here.

Christmas passed like a breath held too long, relief welling up to fill the emptiness it left behind. The family resumed the routine of ordinary days. Father and the uncles tended the horses. Great-Aunt Lucinda, Great-Aunt Lydia, and Uncle William's wife kept the household running almost as smoothly as ever, in proud defiance of their dwindling resources. Great-Aunt Lucinda often reminded the children how fortunate they were to have the farm, to be self-sufficient when so many others were out of work or in debt. Although they had lost nearly all of their savings when the Waterford Bank failed after the stock market crash, they would never be forced from their lands, even if Bergstrom Thoroughbreds never earned another dime. Business had declined precipitously, but the Bergstrom family had built its fortune raising their prized thoroughbreds, and someday, when the Depression ended, their once wealthy customers would return. That was what Sylvia's father said, and Sylvia believed him.

Still, the family could not make or grow everything they needed — shoes for growing children, farm implements and tools — so for the first time in Sylvia's memory, her father took on work away from Elm Creek

Manor. In the months following his wife's death, Sylvia's father had begun accepting invitations to lecture at agricultural colleges across the state. Sometimes he would leave the farm in Uncle William's care for days at a time, traveling from one college to another, earning modest fees for sharing what he knew about regional cultivars, animal husbandry, and fireblight. Sylvia missed him terribly while he was gone and wished he would invite her to accompany him, but the solitude of travel seemed to do him good. Each homecoming seemed to remind him that although the greatest love of his life had departed forever, there was still much love awaiting him at home, people who cared for him, children who depended upon him, reasons to go on. The money he earned, though it flowed out almost as quickly as he could draw it in, allowed them to feel as if they were regaining their footing little by little, that they would manage until their customers returned.

Sylvia's father often returned home with stories of hard times in the towns and cities beyond the Elm Creek Valley, of bread lines and soup kitchens, of bankrupt farms and closed factories. With each tale, Sylvia felt the desperation and fear of the outside world creeping closer until it seemed as if

Elm Creek Manor stood alone, apart, bathed in sunlight in the tightening eye of a storm.

Once, in late autumn, Father returned home from a trip to Philadelphia, his demeanor quiet and pensive. Long after she was supposed to be in bed, Sylvia stood outside the library door and listened as her father told Great-Aunt Lucinda and Uncle William about a strange encounter with a man at the train station.

"He knew my name, although I had never seen him before in my life," said Sylvia's father. "His shoes and his fine topcoat told me he was no farmer, and although I didn't recognize him from my lecture, he seemed to know a lot about me. He followed me onto the platform, questioning me with direct intent about Elm Creek Manor. Right before my train was due to arrive, he got to the point. 'I don't think there's much market for thoroughbreds in these hard times,' he said. 'It's a good thing you have all that land.'

" 'Not a single acre is for sale,' " I told him.

"He told me he was glad to hear it because he worked for certain men in the city — he didn't offer their names — who wanted to hire a farmer to grow particular crops for them. In exchange for growing, harvesting, and delivery, they would pay ten dollars a bushel over the most recent market value."

"Good heavens," said Great-Aunt Lucinda. "What crop could anyone possibly want so badly?"

"Barley and hops."

Uncle William gave a low whistle. "Who do you think he was? Mickey Duffy? One of the Lanzetti brothers?"

"Could have been," Sylvia's father replied. "He kept his hat brim pulled down and stayed out of the lamplight."

"You should have asked for his autograph just in case."

"The joke seems to be on those unsavory characters," said Great-Aunt Lucinda. "They pinned their hopes on an honest man. You've never broken a law in your life, Fred — as far as I know. Why would they ask you, of all people, to get involved in one of their schemes?"

"He didn't say, but I can guess," said Sylvia's father. "Elm Creek Manor is remote, but still accessible to the city. I'm traveling around giving lectures for peanuts, so it's obvious I could use the money. The point is they did ask me, and we have to decide how to answer."

Great-Aunt Lucinda's gasp made Sylvia

jump. "You mean you didn't turn him down right then and there?"

"It's a family farm, so it's a family decision."

"Well, my answer is no," declared Great-Aunt Lucinda. "Absolutely not. We should have no dealings whatsoever with bootleggers and moonshiners. Ties to organized crime won't bring us anything but trouble."

"It's good money," said Uncle William. "We could sow the north field with half corn for feed, half hops, easy. Think of the money we could earn. It would make up for all our lost income."

"My soul is not for sale at any price," Great-Aunt Lucinda shot back. "If your conscience wouldn't bother you, think of the consequences if we were found out."

"It's not against the law to grow barley and hops," said Sylvia's father.

Great-Aunt Lucinda spoke no further, but Sylvia could imagine her withering glare in reply.

"Then the answer is no," said Sylvia's father. She thought she detected a note of relief in his voice.

"But you said you didn't know the man," said Great-Aunt Lucinda. "How will you contact him?"

"He said he would be in touch."

Uneasiness swept over Sylvia, but Great-Aunt Lucinda held steady: "Perhaps we'll never hear from him. Let's hope he finds someone else to be his patsy."

Autumn turned into winter, and if the man from Philadelphia ever contacted her father, Sylvia did not hear of it. As time passed, she stopped waiting for an unfamiliar car to circle the front drive, stopped fearing a sinister figure at the front door. Although she longed to know for certain whether the gangsters had lost interest in the Bergstrom farm, she could not ask her father without revealing that she had eavesdropped. Nor could she breathe a word to Claudia.

The day after Christmas, Sylvia escaped the lonely confines of the manor, her coat pockets full of apples for her favorite horses. Apples the Bergstroms had in abundance, for the orchards had flourished in glorious indifference to the hard times all around them, to their loss and their grief. Her boots crunched through the icy crust on the snow as she made her way to the stable, holding her hood closed tightly with one mittened hand to keep out the sharp wind.

Suddenly, a few yards ahead of her, a shadow broke away from the stable wall.

Too startled to scream, Sylvia froze in her tracks and stared as the unfamiliar figure of a man shuffled toward her. She took a stumbling step backward, her thoughts flying to the gangster from Philadelphia.

"Don't be scared, miss," the man said gruffly, taking a hesitant step forward, his palms raised. "I didn't mean to scare you. I was just trying to find someplace to wait out the storm is all."

She took in his threadbare layers of clothes, dark stubble on a haggard face, and knew at once that he could not possibly be the man from the train station. "You can't go in the stable," she said, her voice high and thin. "You'll scare the horses."

"All right." He ducked his head and stepped back. "I hear you, miss. I don't want any trouble. I'm just trying to keep warm."

He turned around and headed for the bridge over Elm Creek, back into the woods. "Wait," Sylvia called, then turned and ran to the house without waiting to see if the man obeyed. She burst through the back door and raced through the house until she found her father upstairs in the library, his ledger lying open on the oak desk before him. "There's a man outside," she said breathlessly. "I don't think he's the gangster.

I think he's a hobo."

"I wasn't aware that you were acquainted with either," her father said, as she seized his hand and pulled him to his feet. In another moment they were at the back door, pulling on coats and boots. They found the man just outside, sitting on the back steps.

"Good afternoon," Sylvia's father said, addressing the man with utmost respect.

"Afternoon, sir." The man removed his hat despite the cold wind. "I'll work for a meal. I can clean out stables, milk cows, whatever you need."

"The cows won't need to be milked again until tonight," Sylvia's father said, and Sylvia knew he was thinking that anyone who didn't know the proper times to milk a cow could not have much experience with farm life. "Can you handle a shovel?"

"I have a strong back."

"All right, then." Father opened the door wider. "Come inside to the kitchen and get a bite to eat. Afterwards I'll show you around the stables."

The man came inside — quickly, before Father could change his mind — and tugged off his boots. Sylvia recoiled at the smell and backed off down the hallway, wrinkling her nose. She knew it was rude, but she couldn't help it.

She peeked through the doorway as the man wolfed down everything Great-Aunt Lucinda set before him — eggs and ham, bread, coffee, tomato and corn relish, dried apple pie. He ate every crumb, including a few that fell into his lap or the folds of his grimy scarf. When he finished, he thanked Great-Aunt Lucinda politely and followed Sylvia's father back outdoors.

At supper Father reported that the man had put in a good day's work and might make a decent farmhand even though his last steady job had been as a shoe salesman.

"We can't hire him on," said Uncle William, anticipating his brother's unspoken suggestion.

"We could use the help," Sylvia's father pointed out.

"But we can't afford his wages," said Great-Aunt Lucinda. "It would be wrong to expect him to work only for room and board."

Sylvia thought the hobo would gladly accept such an offer, but the children were expected to stay out of business discussions, so she kept her thoughts to herself. She stole a glance at her sister, who looked horrified at the prospect of that filthy man joining them at their table every day.

"We know nothing about him," said Lydia,

glancing nervously out the window to the barn, where Sylvia's father had told the man he could spend the night. "He says he's a shoe salesman, but what proof do we have of that? He could be on the run from the law. What's a hobo doing this far from the train, anyway? Don't they ride the rails?"

Father fell silent, his gaze shifting to Sylvia, Claudia, and Richard. He studied them for a moment as if weighing a heavy burden. "I think he's just a man fallen on hard times, but you're right, we don't know for certain. I'll let him work for his meals and a place to sleep in the barn as long as he likes, but he stays out of the house and away from the children."

Claudia looked relieved, but Sylvia felt a wave of disappointment. She had never met a real hobo before, and she wanted to hear about riding the rails.

The man left the next morning, after breakfast. Two days later, another man knocked on the back door. He had heard, he said, that a kindly family there would give a man a hot meal and a place to sleep in exchange for chores. Father found work for him in the barn, Great-Aunt Lucinda fed him ham and eggs, and the man spent the night in the hayloft.

"We're not a hotel," Claudia muttered as

she and Sylvia spied on the man through the kitchen window. "We never should have helped that first hobo. Now he's told all his hobo friends about us and they'll never leave us alone."

"Father could never send a man away with an empty stomach," Sylvia replied.

After a day, the second hobo left, and when two days passed with no strangers at the back door, Sylvia began to think their visits had ended. But late in the morning on the last day of the year, a knock sounded as she was helping Great-Aunt Lucinda cut up carrots for soup.

"I'll get it," Sylvia sang out, wiping her hands on her apron and hurrying to the back door before anyone could warn her to keep her distance. On the back steps stood two boys not much older than she and Claudia, huddling together for warmth.

She was too surprised to do anything but stare at them.

"We can do chores," the elder boy said. The younger nodded, his face streaked with dirt.

Sylvia didn't wait for permission. "Come in."

The boys exchanged a glance and followed her to the kitchen. Great-Aunt Lucinda quickly hid her surprise and invited the boys to wash up before sitting down at the table. She sent Sylvia to the cellar for butter and apples, and she quickly put together a meal of bread-and-butter sandwiches, cheese, cold bacon left over from breakfast, milk, and apples. The boys devoured the hasty lunch as if it were a feast.

When they had eaten every bite, Great-Aunt Lucinda instructed the younger boy to sweep out the cellar and sent his older brother outside to scrape ice from the back stairs. They were hard at work when the rest of the family came to the kitchen for lunch.

"Runaways?" Uncle William asked his aunt.

Sylvia, who had chatted with the boys, peeling carrots while they ate, piped up, "Not on purpose. Their dad sent them away."

"Why?" said Claudia. "What did they do?"

"Nothing," said Sylvia. "I think they didn't have enough food at their house, so their parents kept the little kids and sent the big ones away."

"What is this world coming to," said Great-Aunt Lucinda, "when families have to send their children out to fend for themselves? We should take them home at once."

"Who's to say their parents won't turn

them out again?" said Sylvia's father.

Great-Aunt Lucinda, unaccustomed to helplessness, fluttered her hands and made no reply.

Sylvia's father frowned thoughtfully. "We can't have them stay in the barn."

"Heavens, no," said Great-Aunt Lucinda.

"But we can't take them in," said Uncle William.

"Why not?" said Sylvia. "We have enough room."

"Ample space isn't the problem," said Great-Aunt Lucinda, as if the admission pained her.

At once, Sylvia understood. With the business all but defunct, they could not afford two additional mouths to feed. How that must have pained her father, who had always generously shared his family's abundance. How her mother's heart would have broken to turn away someone in need.

"We could take them to the Children's Home in Grangerville," said Great-Aunt Lydia. "The good sisters will see that they have warm beds and enough to eat, and they'll be able to go to school."

"It's the best we can do," said Uncle William.

One by one, the adults at the table nodded their assent.

After lunch, Great-Aunt Lucinda sent the brothers off to take a bath; they obeyed reluctantly, sensing, perhaps, that their fates had taken a sudden turn. Sylvia and Claudia searched the attic for warm winter clothing Uncle William had outgrown, and before long the boys were clean and clad in sturdy wool trousers and soft flannel shirts. There was even a pair of boots for the younger boy.

Uncle William cleared his throat as he gave each boy a dime "for emergencies." Great-Aunt Lucinda wrapped cookies in napkins and tucked them into the boys' pockets. She kissed them each on the brow and quickly disappeared into the kitchen. The boys shifted uneasily, throwing anxious glances at the door as Sylvia's father explained where he was taking them. To prove that everything was all right, he asked Sylvia to accompany them on the drive to Grangerville.

The brothers spoke very little as they traveled along the country road winding through the Elm Creek Valley. Sylvia tried to lift their spirits with cheerful accounts of the sights they passed — downtown Waterford, the Four Brothers Mountains, the swirling waters at Widow's Pining where children were not allowed to swim, the forest where old Indian trails could still be followed for miles from one end of the valley to the other.

She had run out of things to say by the time they passed the first sign for Grangerville. Soon afterward, her father pulled up in front of a stately three-story red brick building not far from the center of town. The younger boy let out a sound that might have been a whimper, but his brother quickly hushed him.

Inside, a gray-haired nun in a stiff black-and-white habit welcomed the boys and took down their names and ages. Sylvia, longing for signs of happy children, heard footsteps and laughter overhead. Two girls ran past in simple pinafores, their hair neatly braided. At the sight of the sister, they slowed to a walk, pausing to nod a welcome to the boys.

Sylvia's father pressed a crisp bill into the nun's hand. "For anything they might need," he said. "Write to me if they require more."

The nun nodded and thanked him graciously. Sylvia's father squeezed her shoulder and led her back outside to the car.

"Do you think they'll be happy there?" Sylvia asked as they drove back to Waterford.

"I hope so," her father said. "I hope they'll stay long enough to give the place a fair chance. They could run off again and find themselves in serious trouble."

As uncertain as Sylvia felt about an orphanage, she knew it was a far better place for the boys than haylofts and boxcars. She hoped the boys would think so, too. She hoped they would find the food as delicious as Great-Aunt Lucinda's and the beds as warm and comfortable as those where she and her sister slept.

"Your mother would have been proud of you today," her father said suddenly. "Those boys were frightened, but you helped them to be brave."

"All I did was talk to them."

"That was precisely what they needed," he said. "Sylvia —" He hesitated. "Sylvia, your mother made the most of her time on this earth. Her kindness and generosity live on. It makes me very happy to see that you are going to be exactly like her in that regard."

He reached over and ruffled her hair, yet what had she done to deserve such praise? Mama would have taken the brothers in. She would have found them rooms with soft beds and warm quilts, and she would have seen that they never went hungry. Mama always found a way.

Sylvia wished she were more like her mother. She knew she was not.

But perhaps she could try to be. On that New Year's Eve before Richard was born, her mother had told her that the New Year presented an opportunity to reflect and to improve oneself. Why shouldn't she resolve to be more like her mother?

When they returned home, Sylvia retrieved her sewing box from the nursery and asked Great-Aunt Lucinda if she could borrow from the aunts' scrap bag. "What are you making?" her great-aunt asked, kneeling on the braided rug and pulling out the bag from behind the old treadle sewing machine Great-Grandma Anneke had brought over from Germany. No one used it anymore, preferring the newer electric model Sylvia's father had bought for her mother, but it remained in a place of honor in the west sitting room as a proud memento of their thrifty, industrious ancestor.

"I want to make some quilts to give to the orphans at the Children's Home," Sylvia answered.

Great-Aunt Lucinda sat back on her heels. "Why, Sylvia, that's a lovely idea. It's also quite a task for one girl to take on all by herself. Would you like some help?"

Sylvia gladly accepted her offer, for Great-Aunt Lucinda could sew twice as fast as she could. The more quilts they made, the more comfortable and snug the orphanage would be, and the more likely the brothers would stay.

As they sorted through their fabrics, Great-Aunt Lucinda found a paper sack full of leftover blocks from various projects dating back years. "I had almost forgotten about these," she said, holding them up for Sylvia to admire. "The quilters of this family hate to throw anything away. Fabric was so difficult to come by when the Bergstroms first came to America that we learned to save every scrap. My mother and Aunt Gerda would no more discard a pieced block than they would leave a sewing machine outside in a rainstorm. 'Waste not, want not,' they always said — and today I'm inclined to believe that was a very good lesson."

Since the pretty blocks brought them much closer to their goal, Sylvia was inclined to believe it, too. After laying the blocks out on the floor and debating the possibilities, she and her great-aunt decided that with the addition of a few more blocks, they would have enough to make four quilts just the right size for a child's bed.

They chose simple blocks — Four-Patches, Pinwheels, Bright Hopes — and cut triangles and squares from the brightest, most cheerful fabrics in the scrap bag. As they sewed the pieces together, Great-Aunt Lucinda told her stories of New Year's holidays from long ago. Most of the tales Sylvia had heard several times before, but her great-aunt always remembered new details with each retelling, so that even familiar stories taught her something new about the first Bergstroms to come to Pennsylvania.

They had been hard at work for an hour when Great-Aunt Lydia, with Richard in tow, came looking for her sister. When told about their project, she offered to join in, and soon several rows of blocks were draped over the back of the sofa, waiting to be sewn together with the older women's quick, deft stitches and Sylvia's steady, careful ones.

Claudia must have wondered where everyone was, for eventually she made her way to the west sitting room, drawn by the sound of their voices in laughter. After they explained their task, Claudia regarded Sylvia skeptically, not quite believing her little sister had come up with the idea on her own. "You'll never be able to make enough quilts for every orphan who needs one," she said, lingering in the doorway.

"That doesn't mean she shouldn't do what she can," said Great-Aunt Lucinda, before Sylvia could think of a retort. "Even if she makes only one quilt, that's one more child who will feel warm and loved."

"With our help, she'll make more than one," added Great-Aunt Lydia. "I'm quite proud of our efforts, if I do say so myself. From blocks that were abandoned and forgotten, we are creating objects of beauty, warmth, and comfort. I wish I had resolved to be more frugal and charitable in the coming year, because that's a New Year's resolution I'm already keeping."

She and Lucinda laughed merrily together, as only fond sisters can. Sylvia watched them enviously, not daring to look at Claudia, certain they would never get along so well.

"You may join us if you like," said Great-Aunt Lucinda, but Claudia replied that she would much rather help Aunt Nellie make supper. After she left, Lucinda said, "It's not too late, you know."

"It's not?" said Sylvia.

"Of course not. It's only New Year's Eve. We can still resolve to be more frugal and charitable in the year ahead."

"Oh." Sylvia frowned at her quilting,

disappointed. She had assumed Great-Aunt Lucinda meant it was not too late to befriend Claudia, to become as close as sisters were meant to be, as Lucinda and Lydia were.

Lucinda grimaced and paused in her work to flex her fingers. Her arthritis bothered her in cold weather, and although warm compresses helped, she complained that she couldn't get anything done with her hands wrapped in steaming dishcloths. "I don't see how we can be any more thrifty than we have been," she said, taking up her needle again.

"We could use tea leaves twice, like Bitsy always wanted us to," said Lydia, smiling. Sylvia remembered how Grandma used to urge everyone to squeeze every last drop of tea from the leaves in the strainer, and how Great-Aunt Lucinda, who loved a strong brew, had always added new leaves when Grandma wasn't watching. Suddenly Sylvia felt a pang of remorse so sharp that she had to put down her sewing. Grandma had never made the journey to her mother's homeland, as Sylvia had resolved for her years before. Except in her imagination, she never saw those blazing fireballs light up the New Year's night sky.

"I miss Grandma," she said.

"We do, too," said Great-Aunt Lydia softly, and Great-Aunt Lucinda nodded.

Great-Aunt Lucinda sat lost in thought for a moment, but then she smiled, tied a knot in her thread, and cut it with a quick snip. "I remember stories Bitsy used to tell us about New Year's Eves her father celebrated," she said. "When she first married our brother, she was homesick for her own family's traditions, and telling us about them helped bring her parents closer. They had quite a raucous time, to hear her tell about it."

"I know," said Sylvia. "Swinging fireballs in Scotland. She told me all about it."

"Those are the stories from her mother's side of the family," said Great-Aunt Lydia. "Her father — your great-grandfather — was born in Wales."

Sylvia was instantly captivated. She had heard many stories of Great-Grandfather Hans, founder of Elm Creek Manor, but she could not remember ever hearing about a Welsh great-grandfather.

"Some of the traditions your great-grandfather celebrated in Wales were similar to those your great-grandmother enjoyed," said Great-Aunt Lucinda. "All debts were to be paid, for example, but in Wales there was another twist: If the debtor failed to repay those he owed, he would be fated to be in debt for the rest of the year. It was also considered very bad luck to lend anything on New Year's Day, even something as simple as an egg or a penny."

"I suppose there would be ways around that, to help someone in need," remarked Great-Aunt Lydia, rising to add a completed block to the communal pile on the sofa. "Just call it a gift. If you have no intention of being repaid, that should divert the bad luck."

"You sound just like Bitsy, trying to untangle a knot of superstitions," Great-Aunt Lucinda declared, laughing. To Sylvia, she added, "Debts had to be paid and homes had to be cleaned because your behavior on New Year's Day foretold how you would act throughout the year. If you rose early and got right to work on the first morning of the New Year, you would be industrious for the next twelve months. If you fought with your sister, well, you would probably be argumentative the whole year through."

"That would explain a lot," said Great-Aunt Lydia, with a sidelong glance at Sylvia. "Perhaps we should consider keeping the girls apart on New Year's Day from now on, Lucinda. What do you think?"

184

"It's worth a try."

Sylvia ignored the banter. "Did my great-grandfather's family eat anything special for good luck?"

"Not that I know of," said Great-Aunt Lucinda, "but they did follow another interesting custom called Letting In. It claimed that the first visitor of the New Year brought luck into the house, good or bad."

"I've heard of that," said Sylvia. "Grandma said that in Scotland it's called First Footing. A talk, dark-haired, handsome man like my father brought the best luck of all, but ladies expecting babies or new brides were good, too."

"Not in Wales, they weren't," said Great-Aunt Lucinda. "Oh, a handsome dark-haired man would be welcome, but a woman was the last person you wanted as your first visitor of the New Year. She might be a witch, and a group of young boys would have to run through every room of the house to break her spell, just in case."

Sylvia felt vaguely affronted. "What if the woman is your neighbor, and she just came over to wish you a Happy New Year, and you know she definitely isn't a witch? What if she's your cousin, coming to visit for the holidays? Couldn't that be good luck, too?"

"Not according to the tradition, I'm

afraid," said Great-Aunt Lydia.

"It doesn't seem fair."

"It's not fair," said Great-Aunt Lucinda. "The Welsh tradition on the day after Christmas is even worse. Young men and boys were permitted to take holly branches and slash the arms and legs of their female servants until they bled. Can you imagine being a maid or a cook's helper in those days? Christmas would be a day of dread because of what was in store the day after."

"The grown-ups let them do that?"

"I suppose most of them did, or the custom wouldn't have endured so long."

"That's terrible," said Sylvia. She couldn't believe such naughtiness would be tolerated in children. "I hope my great-grandfather didn't hurt anyone like that."

"I think it's highly unlikely that our branch of the family had any servants to torment," said Great-Aunt Lydia. "They were more likely to be on the receiving end."

"Maybe that's why they came to America," said Sylvia.

Her great-aunts laughed. "There was probably more to their decision than fearing injury on the day after Christmas," said Great-Aunt Lucinda. "But I suppose the inequality and tolerance of ill treatment of the lower classes by the wealthy might have played a part."

"My sister, the philosopher," said Great-Aunt Lydia fondly. "You take after Great-Aunt Gerda."

"If only my apple strudel was as good as hers."

"No one's apple strudel will ever be as good as Great-Aunt Gerda's, but don't let that stop you from trying. We'll be happy to eat your attempts."

Both sisters broke into laughter. Richard looked up at them from his toys, grinning happily, certain that he was responsible for their mirth. He usually was, but this time Sylvia knew the great-aunts' joy came from the shared bond of sisterhood and from the satisfaction of knowing they were doing good work in the company of loved ones. Although they had experienced losses and disappointment in past years, they did not despair, but faced the future with courage and hope.

Suddenly Sylvia decided on her own New Year's resolution. "Didn't Grandma say that when she was a girl, their custom was to clean the house so that the New Year would offer a fresh, new start?" said Sylvia. "From now on, every New Year's Eve, I'm going to clean out my sewing basket and my scraps and I'm going to make at least one useful thing to give to someone else."

Her aunts praised her resolution and promised to do all they could to help her keep it, that year and every year she lived at Elm Creek Manor.

"You'll be able to help me a long, long time," promised Sylvia. "I'm never leaving home."

The great-aunts exchanged a smile. "What if you meet a nice young man and decide to marry?" asked Great-Aunt Lydia.

Sylvia was surprised they had to ask. When she married, she would bring her husband home to live at Elm Creek Manor with the rest of the family, just as her father did when he married her mother. Elm Creek Manor was the home of her heart, the only home she would ever love. Any man she married would have to understand that.

Since they had no party planned for the evening, no Sylvester Ball to attend, no sugar cone for *Feuerzangenbowle,* and no confectioner's sugar for *Pfannkuchen,* Sylvia and her family had a sewing bee instead. Richard played with toys on the floor or climbed from one lap to another, begging for stories and cuddles. They paused only for supper, and when the great-aunts told Sylvia's father about her New Year's resolution and her plans to make quilts for the Children's Home, he ruffled her hair as he had earlier that day and said, "We'll take the quilts over as soon as you finish." Knowing how he used the automobile as little as possible to conserve gasoline, Sylvia glowed with pride, recognizing his offer as a sign of his approval.

After that, Claudia could not hang back while the others joined in to help. They moved the quilting bee to the ballroom, the site of so many happier New Year's celebrations of days gone by, and sat by the fireside sewing, telling stories, and reminiscing. Not wanting to be excluded from the impromptu party, the men kept the women company, popping corn over the fire, telling jokes, and making outlandish resolutions for the year ahead. "I'll sell one hundred horses," Uncle William promised. "I'll grow two hundred bushels of hops and another two hundred of barley." Everyone laughed as Lucinda feigned outrage and swatted him with a quilt block, but Sylvia wondered how many of them understood the reference.

Settling beside her father on the sofa, Sylvia told him what she had learned about her Welsh ancestors. "Your Grandma told me those stories when I was a boy," he said, and Sylvia realized that just as she had lost a mother and a grandma, so had her father lost his own mother and the wife he loved beyond all others. She had thought only of her own grief, forgetting his. Since her death, only upon Richard would he bestow a rare smile.

At Christmas, he had been too overcome by painful memories of happier days to endure a celebration. But he chose to pass New Year's Eve by the fireside with his family, amending the great-aunts' stories of Sylvia's great-grandfather and revealing a tradition called Calennig. Very early on New Year's morning, Sylvia's great-grandfather and other young boys would procure a fresh evergreen twig and a pail of water. From dawn until noon the boys traversed the village, dipping the twig into the water and sprinkling the faces of neighbors out and about. In return, they would be rewarded with Calennig, or "small gifts" of coins or fruit. If they came to a house where the occupants were still asleep, they sprinkled the doorways instead, singing songs or reciting chants that welcomed the New Year.

"They got treats for splashing grown-ups with cold water in the middle of winter?" asked Claudia, dubious.

"What about the girls?" said Sylvia. "You said the boys went through the villages. You meant boys *and* girls, right?"

Her father shook his head. "My mother said young boys, not boys and girls. I guess little girls weren't interested in mischief. They probably preferred to stay home and help their mothers cook breakfast."

Sylvia caught the look that passed between the great-aunts, the knowing gaze heavenward that said they doubted the little girls' preferences had anything to do with it, and that they didn't expect a man to understand. But then her father's eyes twinkled knowingly. Sylvia smothered a giggle, but her heart welled over with happiness. If her father could joke and tease, perhaps one day he would laugh again.

The family sewed and talked and remembered bygone days and departed loved ones until the clock struck midnight. The New Year had begun, offering a fresh start, a new beginning. Sylvia said a silent prayer that the year ahead would be kinder to them than the one before, that the family would know prosperity and peace, and that time would ease the ache in their hearts.

The next day they ate pork and sauerkraut and the women quilted from morning until nightfall. By the time Sylvia went to bed, two hours past her usual bedtime, the Bergstrom women had finished four quilts, each just the right size to comfort a child.

True to his word, the next day Sylvia's father drove her to the Children's Home in Grangerville. Sylvia presented the quilts to the supervising nun and promised to make more quilts, as many as they needed, though it might take her a few years. When her father asked about the two brothers, Sylvia held her breath, afraid that the nun would shake her head sadly and say that the boys were unhappy, or worse yet, that they had run away. But instead she reported that they were settling in fine; they got along well with the other children, followed the rules, and did their chores. She had written to their parents in care of the post office in the boys' hometown, but she was not hopeful of a reply. "Sometimes the parents have moved on by the time their children make their way to us," she explained, with a gentle turn of her hand that suggested both loss and forgiveness. "Other times, I imagine, they are too fearful or ashamed to write back, or they don't know how to read or write. That's if they ever receive the letters we send. I'm sure some of our children are not entirely honest when they tell us where they came from. Far too many have good reason to fear their parents' finding them."

The nun kept her eyes firmly on Sylvia's

father's, not sparing a glance of misgivings for Sylvia as adults often did when they forgot themselves and spoke of adult concerns in front of children.

"I would give the boys a home if I could," her father said. "My wife passed on a few months ago, and my business is failing. I have three children of my own. It — it wouldn't be possible for me to take in two more."

The nun lowered her gaze and nodded. "Of course. I understand."

He dug into his overcoat pocket and pulled out a folded bill. "For the boys," he said, pressing it into her hand. "When I can do more, I will."

"You've already done a great deal." This time, the nun turned her smile upon Sylvia and gave the folded quilts a pat. "Both of you. God bless for your generosity. I know you won't forget our children."

Sylvia's father took her by the hand and led her back out to the car. As they left Grangerville, Sylvia summoned her courage. "Father?"

"Yes, Sylvia?"

"You said the business is failing." She bit the inside of her lip to keep from crying. "Is it?"

Her father was silent for a long moment.

"It hasn't failed yet."

Sylvia never forgot the boys they left behind that day, or the other lost and abandoned children, or the nuns who watched over them. As the Great Depression wore on, whenever she felt sorry for herself, frustrated by made-over hand-me-down clothes, disappointed by the lack of treats and pleasures that had filled her early years with delight, she swallowed her complaints and forced herself to imagine how much worse off she could have it, if not for the family who loved her, if not for the farm.

Years later, after the nation climbed back on to its feet and their wealthy customers returned as her father had always promised they would, still she kept her New Year's resolution. Every winter she made several quilts for the Children's Home; every year her father drove her to deliver them and to check in on the boys. One year they arrived to find a different nun running the orphanage, for her predecessor had died. Another time they learned that the younger brother showed great aptitude for carpentry and had been apprenticed to a local craftsman; a year later, they discovered that the older boy had run off to join the army.

Long after she left Elm Creek Manor, when it became a more practical matter to send checks rather than quilts, Sylvia continued to think of the brothers and wonder what had become of them. On New Year's Eve, when she brought out her UFOs and made at least one useful thing to give to someone in need, she imagined them healthy and happy, with families of their own and all the joys of home that had been denied them as children.

After Aruna had taken Sylvia and Andrew through the entire house, the newlyweds thanked her and departed. Sylvia took Andrew's arm as they strolled through Central Park, lifting her face to the gray sky as snowflakes danced lightly against her eyelashes. This year, the New Year's Reflections quilt would become the one useful thing she made for someone else. Had she known, somehow, that she was not making the quilt for herself when she had cut the first pieces? Had she sewn the Four-Patch, Pinwheel, and Bright Hopes into the centers of the Mother's Favorite blocks as a reminder of her childhood resolution? Sylvia still believed Great-Aunt Lucinda's plainspoken truth that one should do whatever one could to bring comfort and hope to others in need, even if, as Claudia had bluntly pointed out, one person's efforts would not be enough to set everything to rights. The New Year was the perfect time to look outward as well as inward, for resolutions did not have to be about self-improvement alone. They could very well reflect a wish to make the world a better place — even if in small ways, even if for only one person.

If Sylvia could reach Amy, if her peace offering could persuade her stepdaughter to let go of her anger and reconcile with her father, it would be the greatest gift of happiness Sylvia could give Andrew. And to Amy, who did not know that her stubbornness would hurt more people than her father. Anger and misunderstanding could destroy a family from the inside out, as conflict forced everyone to take sides. Even refusing to favor one side over the other would be seen as taking a position, until even the unwilling were drawn into the conflict. Sylvia had seen this happen to her own family, and she would not let it happen to Andrew if she could help it, if she could show Amy another way.

When Sylvia and Andrew returned to the 1863 House, Sylvia's emotions swirled as she told Adele about the visit to the old Lockwood home. Even the physical experience of the place had done little to evoke the elusive sense of connection to her mother's past.

"Except in the nursery," she said. "I could imagine my mother sitting on the window seat, embroidering her Crazy Quilt, gazing out at Central Park and longing for . . . something. Or someone. I don't know."

Adele's smile was full of compassionate understanding. "Maybe since you have such indelible memories of your mother at Elm Creek Manor, it's difficult for you to sense her anywhere else."

"I suppose so."

"We found one of the Colcrafts' quilts when we bought this house," Adele reminded her. "Did your mother leave behind any of her quilts in the Lockwood home?"

"I didn't see any." Her mother's patchwork certainly would have stood out among the Indian décor. "I'm sure Aruna would have mentioned it. I didn't expect to find any of my mother's possessions there. The Bergstroms couldn't even hold on to her quilts. I spent the last few months searching for several my sister sold off decades ago."

"Did you find them?"

"I found her Crazy Quilt in excellent condition for its age, and the new owner sold it to me for what she had paid — plus a week at quilt camp for her daughter-in-law. The quilt my mother had made to celebrate my parents' anniversary had been cut up to make quilted jackets. Andrew bought the last one for me at an art shop in Sewickley." The jacket was pretty in its own way, but the quilt had been a masterpiece. Sylvia could not understand what could have possessed the woman who cut it up. "Just a few days ago, Andrew and I tracked down my mother's long-lost wedding quilt to a traveling exhibit from the New England Quilt Museum. We had searched quilt shops and museums across the country and had tracked down leads from the Internet, and in the end, it was a tip from a quilter staying at our last bed and breakfast that led us to the right place."

"Think of the odds against finding a single quilt after so many years," Adele marveled. "Did you bring the wedding quilt with you?"

"Why, no," said Sylvia. "Even though my mother made the quilt, it isn't mine anymore. My sister sold it long ago. I don't know exactly how it ended up in the hands of the museum, but I can't simply take it from them."

"You could buy it."

"If the museum is willing to sell it, I suppose I could." How wonderful it would be to take the New York Beauty quilt home to

Elm Creek Manor. Sylvia would cherish it always as a memento of her mother, and she would display it for all the quilt camp's guests to enjoy. But should she? As a part of the museum's collection, her mother's wedding quilt would be seen and enjoyed by many more people. It would be properly cared for and preserved for generations to come. Perhaps taking it home for the enjoyment of a relative few was selfish, and offering it freely to the world was what her mother would have wanted.

"I'll have to think about it," said Sylvia.

Adele reached for her purse. "While you're thinking, I know a place that might provide some inspiration. You're sure to meet several quilters eager to offer their opinions whether you want them or not."

While Andrew relaxed in front of the fire with a copy of Adele's manuscript, Sylvia and Adele took a cab to the City Quilter, a quilt shop in Chelsea that Adele promised was the best in New York. Sylvia was inclined to agree; she had visited the shop once, when it first opened, and she had been delighted by the fabric selections and courteous service. To her surprise, when she and Adele entered the shop, salespeople and customers alike greeted her as something of a celebrity. "I loved your quilt *Sewickley*

Sunrise," gushed one woman, her arms overloaded with shopping bags. "I think it's your best work."

"Thank you," said Sylvia, concealing a wince. She knew the woman didn't mean any harm. *Sewickley Sunrise* had won Sylvia many ribbons and now belonged to the Museum of the American Quilter's Society's permanent collection, so it was undoubtedly her best-known quilt. Still, she had made it so long ago that it pained her whenever anyone told her it was her finest creation. Did they honestly believe she had shown no improvement since then, no growth as an artist? *Sewickley Sunrise* would always remain one of her favorite quilts, but she preferred to believe that her most recent work was far superior and that the best was yet to come.

Sylvia and Adele browsed through the rainbow of fabric bolts displayed on the shop walls, and after their selections were cut and folded, Sylvia searched the display case for a spool of thread in a suitable shade of blue. When she brought the New Year's Reflections quilt from her tote bag to match the thread color to the binding fabric, several onlookers quickly clustered around to catch a glimpse of her work-in-progress. When the quilt shop owner suggested she drape the quilt over a table in the classroom so that everyone could have a better look, Sylvia was happy to comply. She hoped Amy would respond to the quilt as warmly as those quilters did, admiring her adaptation of the Mother's Favorite design, the harmonious colors, and the precise piecing. When one customer asked how she had decided which patterns to include in the center of each larger Mother's Favorite block, Sylvia said only that each one reminded her of a New Year of her past — resolutions made and abandoned, opportunities for new beginnings gladly accepted or stubbornly ignored.

As the quilters bent over the quilt, Adele drew close to Sylvia to murmur in her ear. "Your points are so perfect no one would ever know that you'd had a stroke. You should be proud. I know it wasn't easy."

With a jolt, Sylvia suddenly wondered if that was why she had felt compelled to give this particular quilt to Amy, out of the many she could have chosen. Had she subconsciously hoped it would prove to her new stepdaughter that she was perfectly sound, that she had completely recovered from her stroke and would not be a burden to Andrew? Sylvia hoped not, or at least she hoped that Amy would not think so, because that would diminish the beauty of her gift.

Besides, she had stitched most of those blocks long before her stroke, so as proof of her current dexterity and mental acuity, it was flimsy evidence indeed.

Sylvia smiled so that Adele would not realize that the generous praise troubled her. She folded up the quilt and returned it to her tote bag, thanking the onlookers for their kind words and reminding them to visit the Elm Creek Quilt Camp website for more information about the upcoming season of quilt camp. "I hope to see you next summer," she said as she and Adele made their way to the cash register. Several customers called out that she could count on it.

Outside, the sun had come out from behind the clouds, and although the wind was still brisk, Sylvia assured Adele that she felt quite comfortable walking. "Good," said Adele. "I have something to show you."

Mystified, Sylvia strolled along with her friend, up Fifth Avenue back toward Midtown. Surely Adele did not mean to show her the Empire State Building or Rockefeller Center or any of the other obvious tourist stops, which Adele pointed out only in passing. Just as Sylvia's curiosity could bear it no longer, Adele stopped at the corner of a large building in a busy shopping district. "We're here."

Sylvia glanced around, uncertain what distinguished that place from any other in the city. The elegance of the classical architecture was striking, but in that it was not unlike many other buildings they had passed along the way. "Where's here, exactly?"

Adele gestured toward the marble cornerstone. "You might not recognize it, but I think your mother would."

Her heart quickening, Sylvia drew closer to read the bold engraving on the stone. "The Lockwood Building. 1878." She gasped and turned to her friend. "Do you mean —"

"This was the site of your grandfather's store," Adele confirmed. "Lockwood's took up the entire block, once upon a time. The interior has been subdivided and resold many times over since then, but the exterior hasn't been changed since your grandfather's day except for repairs and maintenance."

"I almost can't believe it really exists." Sylvia traced the engraving with a fingertip. "Lockwood's always seemed like nothing more than a setting from a story to me, just like . . ."

"Just like your mother's childhood home?"

Sylvia nodded. "Until this morning, anyway." She stepped back and gazed skyward to take in the entire building her grandfather had built, not caring if she looked like a wide-eyed tourist to the more sophisticated passersby. "One of my mother's favorite memories of this time of year was coming to the store with her father and being allowed to pick out any toy she wanted for Christmas."

"Perhaps this photo was taken on one of those occasions." Adele reached into her bag and pulled out a large padded envelope. "Here's the second part of your surprise. Merry Christmas, a little late. Happy New Year, a little early."

Sylvia pressed a hand to her lips before setting her shopping bags on the sidewalk dusted with snow and accepting the envelope with a trembling hand. She lifted the flap and spied the edge of a photograph, protected between two sturdy pieces of cardboard. Carefully she withdrew a black-and-white photograph of a New York street scene in what appeared to be the early 1900s. A man and woman dressed in turn-of-the-century coats and hats stood with two girls in front of a storefront window emblazoned LOCKWOOD'S DEPARTMENT STORE in elegant script. The elder girl, who looked to be around twelve years old, held her father's hand and beamed into the camera as if caught by surprise, a delightful surprise. The mother stood somewhat apart from her husband at the front of the group, while the younger brought up the rear, peering curiously at the photographer. She wore a dark coat with fur trim around the collar and carried a white fur muff, and her thin legs were clad in heavy black stockings.

Sylvia studied the younger girl's face. In her delicate features, she saw the woman her mother would become. "I have no photographs of my mother as a child," she said. "None except this."

"Not even one?" asked Adele. "I would have assumed the Lockwood family had their photographs taken often. They were considered celebrities in their day."

Perhaps the family had once had many photographs, but Sylvia's mother had brought none with her to Elm Creek Manor. Sylvia was beginning to suspect there was more to her mother's story of her decision to marry Sylvia's father than had been revealed. "Where on earth did you find this picture?"

"In the archives of *The New York Times*. I have a friend on staff. This picture appeared in the society column. I included a printout of the newspaper page in the envelope, if you can tear yourself away from the photo long enough to look."

Sylvia gazed at her mother's family, her voice catching in her throat. "Adele, I don't know how to thank you."

"It's just a reprint, not the original," Adele said, almost apologetically. "They wouldn't part with that. But since it isn't the authentic photo, you don't have to worry about it disintegrating before you can get it home. You also won't have to treat it like a museum piece, with archival matting and protective glass."

Sylvia might not have to, but she would. Reprint or not, this photo of the Lockwood family was the only one she possessed, and she would not trade it for a dozen museum pieces.

CHAPTER FOUR

The next morning at breakfast, the resourceful Adele reported that she had found *Dinner for One* on the Internet. Pleased, the German couple invited the other guests to join them around the computer on New Year's Eve. Only Sylvia and Andrew declined, with some regret, because they would be leaving New York later that day.

They bade their fellow guests good-bye and Happy New Year; they parted from Adele and Julius with warm embraces and promises to get together again soon. They enjoyed a morning of exploring museums, shopping, and savoring a delicious lunch, then they packed up the Elm Creek Quilts minivan and continued on to Amy's home in Hartford, Connecticut.

As Andrew drove, Sylvia once again took up her needle to finish sewing the binding on Amy's quilt. She had not made as much progress during their stay in New York as she had planned, but she hoped to make up for it on the two and a half hour drive.

"Do you think you'll finish it by New Year's Eve?" Andrew asked as they pulled on to I-95.

"I'll take until New Year's Day if necessary," she said, "but I hope I won't offend anyone if I sneak away from family gatherings now and then to work on it."

Amy might prefer, in fact, for Sylvia to leave the family to themselves. It was difficult not to be hurt by the younger woman's sudden disapproval. Amy had liked Sylvia well enough when she and Andrew were dating; Amy had been a gracious hostess whenever the couple visited and she had even asked Sylvia to teach her to quilt. But Amy's friendliness had evaporated the moment she heard of their engagement. Andrew had anticipated this and had decided to break the news to his children in person. First the couple had driven to his son's home in southern California, where Bob and his wife had taken the news with surprise and concern. Although the visit had ended badly, Bob had agreed to say nothing to his sister so that Andrew could be the one to tell her. Andrew had forgotten to secure that promise from Bob's wife, however, so when Sylvia and Andrew returned to Elm Creek Manor, they had found Amy waiting for them.

Andrew frowned and flexed his fingers around the steering wheel. "That's fine with me as long as you're only sneaking off to quilt, and not because anyone has made you feel unwelcome."

"I'm not expecting a warm welcome," Sylvia said. "Please don't feel you have to rush to my defense over the tiniest slights as you did in California."

"You're my wife, and I expect my children to treat you with respect."

"They're more likely to do so if you let them do it on their own terms, and not because you've scolded them into it."

"I guess you're right. Maybe." Andrew tapped the steering wheel thoughtfully. "Maybe we should make a plan. How should we break the news?"

"I don't think we need to worry about how Daniel will take it." Amy's husband had approved of their engagement from the beginning. Sylvia and Andrew were counting on him to help bring Amy around. "I think it's best to tell her right away, but delicately. We should be sensitive to her feelings, but at the same time she needs to know that there's no longer any point in trying to convince us to cancel our plans to marry."

"It's too late for that," said Andrew, reaching for her left hand and pressing it to his lips. Her thimble fell into his lap, and she laughed as she retrieved it. Andrew's smile faded into a sigh. "I don't understand these kids. Why shouldn't they want us to get married? We love each other. They ought to be happy for us."

"They should be," said Sylvia. "Unfortunately, in my experience, people in love almost always stumble over objections thrown in their path by one side of the family or another. 'The course of true love never did run smooth,' as the poet said."

"I wouldn't say 'almost always,' " said Andrew. "Do you really believe that?"

"Almost every marriage I know of has offended someone," said Sylvia. "And I'm not talking about envious former sweethearts, but friends and family who ought to have the couple's best interests at heart. Sarah and Matt McClure, for example."

Andrew shrugged in acknowledgment. Sarah's mother's antipathy for her son-in-law was as infamous in Elm Creek Quilts circles as it was perplexing, for Matt was a fine young man. "All right, that's one."

"My parents," said Sylvia. "Agnes and my brother."

"Who objected to their marriage?"

"Her parents," said Sylvia. "Don't you remember? And . . . I admit I did, too."

Andrew grinned. "That's because you didn't want to share your baby brother with anyone."

"That's not the reason. They were too young."

"Richard was about to be shipped out," Andrew protested. "It was wartime. Lots of young couples rushed off to get married back then."

"Fair enough." Sylvia knew he was right, and if Agnes and Richard had not seized that moment, they never would have married. "John Colcraft and Harriet Beals."

"Who?"

"The couple who built the 1863 House."

Andrew laughed. "Okay, that's three, spanning two centuries. I can't call that a trend."

"My cousin Elizabeth and Henry Nelson." Sylvia couldn't admit that she was the only person who had objected to that pairing, but Andrew had heard enough of her childhood stories to figure that out for himself. "My sister and Harold Midden."

Andrew scowled, for he had good reason to dislike Harold. He had been outraged to learn that Claudia had married him.

211

"Sometimes it's right to object to a marriage."

"Your son and daughter think this is one of those times."

"They're wrong."

"I know that, dear. You're preaching to the choir."

Andrew fell silent, lost in thought, and Sylvia returned her attention to the New Year's Reflections quilt. Even if Andrew couldn't detect a trend, Sylvia could, and she couldn't ignore it. It seemed that nearly all married couples of her acquaintance had encountered some disapproval of their marriage, and sometimes Sylvia herself had been the source. She would never change her mind regarding Harold Midden's unsuitability, but in hindsight, she wished she had been more generous to Agnes and Richard and to Elizabeth and Henry. She could not help wondering if her resolute lack of acceptance then had come around to haunt her now.

She might have believed it, except for one thing. Out of all the couples she had known throughout her life, one had been blessed with a marriage welcomed with unabated joy on both sides of the family.

The fortunate couple had been Sylvia herself and her first husband, James.

They had met at the State Fair when Sylvia was sixteen and James eighteen. Although James's father was her father's business rival, the men shared a mutual respect and approved when James began courting Sylvia. When they married and James came to Elm Creek Manor to live, as Sylvia had planned since childhood, Mr. Compson celebrated their happiness even though it meant that his son had joined the family business of his chief competitor. The Compson family never failed to treat Sylvia as a beloved daughter and sister, and the Bergstroms extended the same love and acceptance to James.

The first years of their marriage were as blissful as any young couple could have hoped for, the only unfulfilled promise the absence of children. But they had plenty of time, they told each other, years and years in which the blessing of a baby might be granted to them.

Then the war came. Richard and Andrew, whom in those days Sylvia thought of only as her brother's friend, left school and enlisted. In hopes of looking after them, James promptly enlisted, as did Harold, Claudia's longtime suitor, perhaps bowing to pressure from his fiancée. Within weeks of the men's deployment to the South

Pacific, Sylvia learned that she was pregnant.

Sylvia, Claudia, and Agnes waited out the lonely, anxious months together at Elm Creek Manor. Sylvia and her father, who had all but retired from Bergstrom Thoroughbreds after teaching James all he knew, held together the family business as best they could. Winter came, and although it was difficult with their loved ones facing unimaginable dangers so far away, those left behind managed to find joy and hope in the Christmas season and faced the New Year with resolve. Nineteen forty-five would be the year the war ended and the boys came home, they told one another as they toasted the New Year, but their voices were wistful. Nineteen forty-five was the year Sylvia's child would be born and Claudia would marry. Their only resolutions were to keep up their courage, to pray for peace, to make any sacrifice they could to speed the end of the brutal war.

But 1945 saw the destruction of all their hopes. A few months after Christmas, James died attempting to save Richard's life after a horrific attack on a beach in the South Pacific. The shock of the news sent Sylvia into premature labor. Her daughter succumbed after struggling for life for three days. Unable to bear the shock of so much loss, her father collapsed from a stroke.

Sylvia remembered little of those dark days. Devastated by grief, she remembered lying in a hospital bed, holding her baby's small, still body and weeping. She recalled begging the doctors to release her so she might attend her father's funeral. She remembered calling out for James and when he did not come, screaming at Agnes until her sister-in-law wept.

Eventually Sylvia was released from the hospital. At first, the numbness of shock protected her, but all too soon it receded, to be replaced by the most unbearable pain. Her beloved James was gone, and she still did not know how he had died. Her daughter was gone. She would never hold her again. Her darling little brother was gone. Her father was gone. The litany repeated itself relentlessly in her mind until she believed she would go mad.

The war ended. Andrew went home to family in Philadelphia, while Harold returned to Elm Creek Manor thinner, more anxious, and aged beyond the months he had spent in the service. As if to cast off the grief and sorrow shrouding the home, Claudia threw herself into their wedding plans. As her maid of honor, Sylvia was expected to help, but although she wanted to please her sister, she often forgot the tasks Claudia assigned to her. Sylvia's heart was not in the celebration. She had lost her heart when she lost James and her daughter.

A few weeks before the wedding, Andrew paid an unexpected visit on his way from Philadelphia to a new job in Detroit. Sylvia was glad to see him. Like Harold, Andrew had changed. He walked with a limp and sat stiffly in his chair as if maintaining army regulations. He was kind and compassionate to the grieving women, but he coldly shunned Harold, who seemed all too willing to avoid Andrew in turn. Though Sylvia would have thought the men unified by wartime experiences, perhaps, she decided, seeing each other dredged up unbearable memories.

It fell to Andrew to tell Sylvia how her brother and husband had died, although he warned her she would find no comfort in the truth. Haltingly, every word paining him, he described the terrible scene he had witnessed from a bluff overlooking the beach, how Richard had come under friendly fire, how James had raced to his rescue, how he would have succeeded with the help of one more man, how Harold had hidden himself rather than risk his own life.

Andrew begged for her forgiveness. He had run straight down the bluff to the beach where his friends lay dying, knowing that he would never make it in time. Sylvia held him as he wept, the heart she thought she had lost hardening to cold stone within her. She told Andrew she forgave him for his sake, but there was nothing to forgive. The blame was not his. Andrew had tried to save her brother and husband. He had risked his own life despite knowing that he would likely fail. Harold had not even tried.

Andrew left Elm Creek Manor the next morning, and Sylvia brooded over the burden of Harold's secret. As the days passed and the plans for the wedding progressed, Sylvia eventually realized that she could not possibly allow her sister to marry Harold unaware of his role in James's and Richard's deaths. But to Sylvia's astonishment, Claudia accused Sylvia of lying out of jealous spite and insisted that the wedding would go on. Sylvia left Elm Creek Manor that day, unable to bear the sight of the man who had allowed her husband and brother to die, unable to live with a sister who embraced a lie.

Into two suitcases she packed all she could carry — photographs, letters from Richard and James, the sewing basket she had received for Christmas the year before her mother died. Everything else she left behind — beloved childhood treasures, favorite books, unfinished quilts. Everything except memories and grief.

She left the manor not knowing where she would go. She walked miles to the bus station in Waterford, where she purchased a ticket to Harrisburg. She spent the night at Aunt Millie and Uncle George's hotel, conscious of their surprise at her unexpected appearance and their concern for her fragile state. She burned with rage and grief, but she told them nothing of Andrew's devastating account of Harold's betrayal of the Bergstrom family, the family he did not deserve to join.

Mercifully, her aunt and uncle were satisfied with her explanation that she needed time away from the manor, and they did not inquire too insistently about her itinerary. Instead they shared recent letters from Elizabeth, cheerful accounts of Henry and the children and Triumph Ranch. The bright sunshine and warm breezes of southern California seemed impossible in a world without Richard and James and her daughter and father.

As she drifted off to sleep that night, Sylvia considered taking a train west as Elizabeth had done so many years before. Her cousin would take her in. Sylvia could work herself into exhaustion on the ranch and drop off to a dreamless sleep every night. Love for her young niece and nephews could fill the void in her heart. But when she woke in the morning, Sylvia knew she could not find refuge with any Bergstrom, even one as far away as Elizabeth. A Bergstrom would send word to Claudia and urge her to return home, and that Sylvia could not bear.

The next day she thanked her aunt and uncle for their kindness and bought a train ticket to Baltimore.

She had phoned ahead, so her mother-in-law was waiting for her on the platform, dressed in black, clutching her handbag anxiously. Sylvia disembarked and almost fell into her arms. "There, there, dear," Mrs. Compson murmured, patting her on the back. "It's all right. Don't worry about anything. We'll take you home."

James's father was waiting in the car, but he leaped out to help her with her luggage. Her throat constricted at the sight of him, so like her James, tall and dark-haired, with blue eyes and a smile that warmed her to her very core. Mr. Compson did not smile now and his face was haggard with grief.

She had not seen her in-laws since the funeral. They seemed to have aged decades in a few months.

Mrs. Compson sat beside Sylvia in the back seat of the Packard as Mr. Compson drove them to their horse farm on the Chesapeake Bay about twenty-five miles southeast of the city. "We've fixed up Mary's room for you," she said. "We hope you'll be comfortable there."

Sylvia's sister-in-law had graduated from the University of Maryland a few months after the attack on Pearl Harbor. While her brothers were at war, she had married a congressman and moved to Washington. At James's funeral she had grieved silently, clutching her husband's arm and staring into the distance.

"I'm sure I will be." Sylvia's voice sounded hollow, unfamiliar. On her last visit to the Compson farm, she and James had stayed in his old room. She was grateful Mrs. Compson had known not to put her there.

Not once did the Compsons ask her why she had come or how long she planned to stay. When the white fences and green pastures of the farm came into view, Sylvia felt a gentle whisper of peace upon her soul, a promise that one day she would be able to remember James's smile or his touch upon her skin without feeling as if her life had ended with his.

Compson's Resolution, six hundred acres of neatly fenced pasture, rolling forested hills, and cultivated farmland, had been in the Compson family since the eighteenth century. The name of the farm came from the settlement of a border dispute with the farmer who owned the acres to the northwest of the Compson property. The Compsons still lived in the two-hundred-year-old brown stone farmhouse with a Gambrel roof that their first ancestor in Maryland had built. Unlike the Bergstroms, who had added an entire wing to the original homestead farmhouse as the family prospered, the Compsons had brought modern conveniences to the interior but kept the footprint of the house essentially unchanged.

Sylvia was accustomed to life on a horse farm, and she soon fell into the rhythm of the Compson household. She rose early to help Mrs. Compson prepare breakfast for the family and the hired hands; she washed clothes and cleaned house; she fed chickens and pigs and tended the kitchen garden. Her mother-in-law appreciated Sylvia's help, for in Mary's absence, the housework had fallen on her shoulders alone. "I'm happier still for your company," she said, pressing a soft, plump hand to Sylvia's cheek. Her kindness brought tears to Sylvia's eyes. How could Mrs. Compson, wracked with grief for the loss of James and her grandchild, bustle about with such brisk, cheerful authority? Perhaps knowing that two of her sons had returned safely home from the war in Europe and that Mary was expecting a child gave her purpose.

Without James, without Elm Creek Manor, Sylvia felt adrift, her only tether to this world the love and kindness of James's parents.

She was most content out of doors, helping Mr. Compson with the horses. Although he and the stable hands would have managed fine without her, whenever Sylvia appeared at the corral, her father-in-law invariably found a horse that needed to be exercised. Riding alone on the trails that criss-crossed Compson's Resolution, resting by the old farm wharf to watch ships on the Chesapeake, Sylvia let go of her grief and soaked in the beauty of a swift horse and blue water and fertile land. But at night she would dream of James and wake up sobbing. Another day without him had begun.

Autumn brought golden hues and crisp sunrises to the farm. Every morning Sylvia wept less; each day she felt less likely to break at the slightest touch. One afternoon, as she and Mrs. Compson peeled apples for a pie, Sylvia reflected upon the apple orchard at Elm Creek Manor and wondered how Claudia and Harold had managed the harvest.

She did not realize she had spoken aloud until Mrs. Compson gently said, "You could return home and find out."

"I can't." Sylvia shook her head. "I can't ever go back. You don't understand."

"I might," Mrs. Compson said, "if you told me why you left."

Sylvia hesitated. Would it be cruel to burden James's mother with the truth of her son's unnecessary death? Mrs. Compson had embraced her with kindness and unconditional acceptance. Sylvia could not bear to bring her any more pain.

Mrs. Compson set down her paring knife and took Sylvia's hand in her own. Her grip was firm and steady. "Nothing you could possibly tell me about James could be worse than losing him," she said. "If I survived that, I can withstand hearing whatever is so terrible it drove you from the home you love."

Sylvia closed her eyes as she retold Andrew's story, but that did not shut out the images seared into her memory as if she, too, had witnessed the terrible scene. Then she explained how she had confronted Claudia, and how her sister had chosen Harold over her family, and why Sylvia could never return as long as they lived in the home where she had known so much happiness with the men Harold had been unwilling to save.

When every word had drained from her, Mrs. Compson groped for the kitchen stool and sank down upon it, weeping twin rivulets of tears without making a sound. Suddenly she took a deep, shuddering breath. "You have only Andrew's account of what happened that day."

"I've known Andrew since childhood," Sylvia responded. "He loved Richard like a brother. He would have no reason to lie, and I trust him implicitly."

Mrs. Compson studied her hands in her lap for a long moment in silence. "You don't know that Harold could have saved them," she said. "You don't know for certain that James would have been able to rescue Richard if Harold had only helped him. Harold might have gone to their aid only to be caught by the second explosion, as my son was."

"Andrew told me what James shouted to

224

Harold before he was killed." Sylvia's voice trembled. "James thought he could save Richard with Harold's help. Andrew thought so, too. But you're right, we'll never know for certain because Harold didn't even try."

"He might have known it would have been in vain," said Mrs. Compson. "He might have seen that second plane coming and known that coming out from cover would be suicide. We can't possibly know what was in his heart."

"How can you excuse what he did?" said Sylvia. "And what he didn't do? Your son is dead because of Harold's cowardice."

Mrs. Compson's shoulders slumped, weary to her soul. "It might not have been cowardice. And my son might have died anyway."

Sylvia could not believe what she was hearing. "How can you not be angry? How can you not hate him?"

"Because it would do me no good." Mrs. Compson looked up at her, a new fierceness in her eyes. "It would not change what happened. Hatred and anger will not bring my son back. They would only destroy me, the way they're clearly destroying you."

Sylvia shook her head, unable to reply. Mrs. Compson was a good woman, too good, perhaps, to understand how wrong she was. Harold deserved Sylvia's hatred, and anger was the only thing that kept her on her feet.

Though Sylvia had told her mother-in-law she would never return to Elm Creek Manor, Mrs. Compson must have thought she heard a quiet note of longing for home in her voice. A few days after Sylvia told her Andrew's story, Mrs. Compson began slipping reminders of Elm Creek Manor into their conversations, whereas she had always avoided the topic before. As they canned tomatoes, she inquired about the Bergstroms' favorite varieties and preparation methods. When Mr. Compson sold a prized yearling, she wondered aloud if the Bergstroms would have demanded a higher price. Sylvia usually offered simple answers, but Bergstrom Thoroughbreds and Elm Creek Manor had been a part of her life for too long for her to feign indifference to them now. She found herself wishing for news of the family business and the estate she once believed would be her home forever, but curiosity could not compel her to write to Claudia. She knew she could not speak to her sister without hurling accusations of betrayal. The very thought of Harold sleeping beneath the roof of Elm

Creek Manor while James, Richard, her father, and her daughter slept forever so filled her with revulsion that she was not even tempted to pick up a pen.

All through that beautiful autumn, Sylvia worked alongside the Compson family. Gradually she found contentment in the routine, in the company, in the rhythm of the days and the satisfaction of the harvest. Then one day, Mrs. Compson declared that she and Sylvia deserved a holiday, and she invited Sylvia to accompany her to a luncheon at a friend's home in Baltimore. "You'll have a lovely time," Mrs. Compson persisted when Sylvia was reluctant to leave the peaceful sanctuary of Compson's Resolution. "My friends are delightful company, and our hostess has some family heirlooms I know you'll find very interesting."

In spite of herself, Sylvia was intrigued, so she agreed to the outing. A Wednesday morning in early November found her beside Mrs. Compson in the black Packard driving northwest into the city. Her friend, Mrs. Cass, had invited several ladies to gather at her grand house in what Sylvia surmised was one of Baltimore's most fashionable neighborhoods. The women welcomed Mrs. Compson and Sylvia warmly and offered Sylvia their condolences in murmurs, as if her grief were a carefully concealed secret. Sylvia was the youngest present by decades, and the only widow among the wives of doctors, lawyers, and businessmen.

Sylvia grew increasingly ill at ease as the other women discussed their husbands and children and household conflicts, for she had lost her husband and had never raised a child and had abandoned her home. She tried to nod and murmur appropriate phrases when an answer was required, but through no fault of their own, the other women made Sylvia feel like an indulged child sent to dancing school in a starched dress to learn how to mimic the mannerisms of grown-ups. The leek soup was flavorful, the crab cakes a new and unexpected pleasure, but although Sylvia smiled and conversed and hid her discomfort as well as she knew how, she could not wait for the luncheon to end. She longed for the sanctuary of the Compson stables, of the wooded riding trails, of the comforting presences of lighthouses overlooking the Chesapeake Bay.

After the meal, Mrs. Cass led her guests into a parlor for coffee and more chat. Sylvia longed for a moment alone with Mrs. Compson so she could beg to be taken home, but she knew that Mrs. Compson would kindly but firmly refuse. Her impeccable manners would not permit her to slight their hostess, and she was convinced a change of scene would do Sylvia good. A new riding trail on the Compson estate was all the change of scene Sylvia wanted. The sympathetic gazes and gentle words of the Baltimore ladies were excruciating.

In the parlor, Mrs. Cass spoke a word to her maid, who disappeared and quickly returned with a bundle wrapped in a muslin sheet. "Your mother-in-law tells me you know a great deal about quilts, Sylvia," Mrs. Cass said as she thanked the maid and took the bundle.

"My mother taught me when I was very young," Sylvia replied. "I grew up watching her and my aunts and grandma quilt together."

"I'm afraid quilting is a lost art among the women of my family," said Mrs. Cass, "but I am fortunate to have several fine examples of my ancestors' handiwork. Although I don't like to brag, I think it's fair to call this quilt a masterpiece."

Sylvia and two other ladies helped Mrs. Cass unfold the bundle. A murmur of appreciation rippled through the room as everyone gathered around to view the quilt.

It was a masterpiece, indeed — twenty-five different appliqué blocks depicting bouquets of spring blossoms gathered in three-looped bows, bowls of fruit with embroidered seeds, symmetrical Turkey red flowers with green stems and leaves, and scenes of eighteenth-century life reproduced in such painstaking detail that they must have been drawn from the quilter's own observations.

"You wouldn't recognize these landmarks, Sylvia, since this is your first visit to Baltimore." Mrs. Cass gestured to several blocks in turn. "This is a famous clipper ship that sailed in the Chesapeake Bay in the 1840s. This is a train from the Baltimore and Ohio Railroad, and this is the Baltimore Basilica on Mulberry and Cathedral streets."

"This is the Peale Museum in its glory days," said another guest, indicating another block. "Before all that dreadful stucco was added."

"It's a truly wonderful quilt," said Sylvia. She had seen quilts made in this style before, but the Bergstrom women had never made any like them as far as she knew. She came closer for a better look. "It looks like the blocks were signed in brown ink and the handwriting . . . yes, a different hand signed each block. Could this be a group quilt?"

"That's what the family stories say," said Mrs. Cass. "My grandmother once told me that this was a Freedom Quilt, made by the women of the family for one of my long-distant great-uncles when he turned twenty-one. For generations we assumed that each block was signed by the quilter who made it, but I've discovered that the record in our family Bible disputes those claims." She gestured to a block in the bottom row. "Hettie Cass would have been only five years old when the quilt was made, and I don't know any child that age who could sew a lyre and floral spray as perfectly as those in her block."

"Is it possible that an older relative didn't want Hettie to be left out of such an important family project, so she made the block on the little girl's behalf?" asked Sylvia.

"I suppose so," said Mrs. Cass thoughtfully. "It seems like the sort of thing a mother or aunt would do."

"I have a similar quilt among my own family heirlooms," said another guest. "The blocks aren't identical to these, of course, but the style is very similar. I like to imagine that our great-grandmothers were friends, and that they quilted together." She smiled at Mrs. Cass.

"Can you imagine how many hours these

231

women must have spent on their master-pieces?" said another guest. "How did they have time to do anything else?"

The other women laughed, and Mrs. Cass said, "They didn't have the amusements and distractions we have today. Quilting with friends might have been the only entertainment available to them."

The implication that women quilted only because they had nothing more interesting to do bothered Sylvia. "Whoever made this quilt was a true artist. I imagine she looked forward to working on it whenever she could slip away from her household chores. I wouldn't be surprised if she turned down invitations just so she could be alone with her fabric and needle."

"It's a pity no one makes quilts like this anymore," said another lady with a sigh.

"Some people do," said Sylvia, surprised that the woman did not know. "Perhaps not in this style, exactly, but intricate and beautiful in their own right."

"I suppose they do, on the farm," another guest acknowledged. "Here in the city, we're much too busy to quilt, and we have so many fine stores where you can buy well-made coverlets at very reasonable prices."

"I don't believe city women are any busier than farm women," said Mrs. Cass, with an amused smile.

"Even in the Elm Creek Valley, the stores carry blankets," said Sylvia. "If all that mattered was keeping warm, we would buy our coverlets, too. The women of my family quilt — they quilted — as a matter of choice, not necessity. We each had our own style, our own favorite colors and patterns, our own unique way of arranging the pieces — even if two of us chose the same pattern and traced the same templates, the quilts we made would be as unique to us as our faces and our voices. My mother's quilts say 'home' to me in a way no blanket from a store ever could."

"I don't know if my daughters could say something so heartfelt about anything I've ever given them," said Mrs. Cass.

"When you put it that way," said the woman who owned a similar quilt, "it sounds like a lovely pastime. I only wish my grandmother had taught me how to quilt."

"I could teach you," said Sylvia.

For the first time, the women regarded her with genuine interest instead of pity. "Could you?" asked one of the guests, a doctor's wife. "It seems so terribly difficult."

"We wouldn't have to begin with a quilt as challenging as this," said Sylvia, indicating Mrs. Cass's heirloom. "We could begin with something simple — a sampler made up of several different blocks in increasing complexity. Working on each block would help you master a particular quilting skill, so that by the time your sampler is finished, you'll be able to approach other patterns on your own with confidence."

The ladies peppered her with eager questions, but Mrs. Cass's voice rose above the chorus: "And how often would you be willing to return to Baltimore to teach us?"

Sylvia threw a questioning glance to Mrs. Compson, who gazed back at Sylvia from beneath raised brows, as curious as the others. She was not going to answer on Sylvia's behalf, so Sylvia took a deep breath and said, "Twice a month, if it's all right with Mrs. Compson."

"Oh, it will be fine with her," said the most outspoken of the ladies. "Isn't it, Josephine?"

"I suppose I can spare her," said Mrs. Compson, smiling. "I believe I'd like to join the quilting bee, too."

Sylvia and the women decided to meet every other Wednesday for lunch and quilting lessons, with each woman taking a turn as hostess. Sylvia advised her new pupils on the supplies they would need to collect for the first lesson, and the room buzzed as they made plans for shopping expeditions.

Everyone bade Sylvia a cheerful farewell as they parted on Mrs. Cass's front walk. As Mrs. Compson turned the Packard toward home, Sylvia's thoughts ran with block patterns and lesson plans. It was a pity they couldn't meet more frequently. Perhaps she could begin each class by introducing a new quilting skill, which the ladies would practice together as a group. She could also leave them with the pattern to another, more advanced block that would reinforce what they had learned in class. Her students would be instructed to finish both blocks before the next class, where Sylvia would inspect them and offer constructive criticism before presenting a new quilting technique.

Suddenly a thought occurred to Sylvia. "Mrs. Cass's friends were nice, but did you notice how they only thought of me as poor Mrs. Compson's widowed daughter-in-law until Mrs. Cass brought out her quilt?"

Mrs. Compson's smile was both amused and knowing. "Did you notice that until Mrs. Cass brought out her quilt, you behaved as nothing more than poor Mrs. Compson's widowed daughter-in-law?"

Sylvia sat back against her seat, chagrined. It was true that she had not really made an effort to get to know any of the ladies, not even Mrs. Cass. Their kindhearted sympathy had been so unbearable that her only aim had been to get through the afternoon. She had not even bothered to learn any of their names. She could not fault them for not seeing the person behind the grief.

Somewhere deep inside her, a spark of realization kindled and burned, a small but steady light. There *was* still a person behind the grief. Until that moment, she had forgotten.

Sylvia spent the next week planning her lessons and preparing patterns. She had tried to teach quilting only once before, when Agnes admired the quilts her sisters-in-law had made and wanted to make a wedding quilt for her and Richard. Sylvia tried to steer her toward basic patterns, but Agnes insisted upon making a Double Wedding Ring, with disastrous results.

Agnes finished only one lopsided ring of her quilt before word came that her new husband had died. Sylvia doubted she would ever make another.

Sylvia wondered what would become of Agnes. After Richard's death, she had stayed on at Elm Creek Manor instead of returning home to her parents, who had not approved of her hasty marriage. Now that Sylvia had left, would Agnes remain at Elm Creek Manor with Claudia and Harold? Sylvia could not imagine the young widow finding any happiness in that arrangement — but she quickly drove her concerns from her thoughts. Agnes was free to make her own decisions. It was none of Sylvia's business whether she stayed to help look after the Bergstrom legacy or if she departed forever as Sylvia had done. Agnes had been a Bergstrom less than a year. She would likely put her girlhood romance behind her and marry again, with, Sylvia hoped, a much happier ending.

The next Wednesday, Sylvia and Mrs. Compson returned to Baltimore and met the aspiring quilters at the home of the doctor's wife. After another delicious lunch, Sylvia demonstrated how to make a simple Nine-Patch block, starting with making templates from cardboard, tracing the shapes on the wrong side of the fabric, cutting and pinning, and sewing the pieces together with a running stitch. Sylvia heard herself echoing the advice and warnings she had heard since childhood from the Bergstrom women: trace the templates with a sharp pencil, make the stitches small and even, mind the seam allowances, don't stretch the fabric out of shape. The Baltimore ladies took eagerly to her lesson, and each finished a twelve-inch block by the end of the afternoon. Sylvia left them with patterns and instructions for a Sawtooth Star block and promised to see them two weeks hence.

The following session, each lady had completed a Sawtooth Star, with the quality ranging from acceptable to expert. Sylvia hesitated as she examined one woman's block, uncertain what to say. While her color choices were among the best in the group, her stitches were uneven and seam allowances almost nonexistent. A child in the Bergstrom family would have been instructed to pick out the stitches and try again. A Bergstrom woman might have passed the block around the quilting circle for a laugh, but then she would have known to start over, perhaps after seeking advice from more experienced quilters in the family.

"What do you think?" asked Mrs. Simmons, after Sylvia studied the block in silence for much longer than it had taken her to evaluate the other women's work.

"You have a wonderful eye for color," said Sylvia.

"Thank you, dear, but what about the sewing?" When Sylvia hesitated, Mrs. Simmons said, "I'm prepared for your honest opinion."

"Well," Sylvia said, "what do you think of your work when you compare your block to what your friends have done?"

"Oh, tell the truth, Doris," teased another lady, a Mrs. Cook. "She knows you didn't do your best but she's too well-mannered to say so."

When the other ladies laughed, Mrs. Simmons gave Sylvia a guilty smile. "I was a bit pressed for time at the end."

"She starting working on the block last night, while the rest of us began the day after our last lesson," another woman called out. "She finished the last seam in the car on the way over."

"Tattletale," retorted Mrs. Simmons, giggling. To Sylvia she added, "I had hoped no one would notice."

Her hastiness certainly explained her results, and Sylvia couldn't help feeling disappointed in her pupil. "I'm sure you see the problems with your block as readily as I do," she said as kindly as she could. "If you put more effort into your next blocks, I'll be able to evaluate your skills more accurately and offer you better guidance next time."

Mrs. Simmons went back to her seat

perfectly content, so Sylvia suspected she felt worse about her first student failure than the student herself. Still, she figured everyone deserved a second chance after one bad decision, so she moved on to the next part of the class and introduced the LeMoyne Star block, one of her favorites. This block would be more challenging than the first two because it required the quilter to "set in" pieces, or sew a piece into an angle between two other pieces.

As the rich colors of autumn faded into the snowy white of winter, the Baltimore Quilting Circle, as the ladies had dubbed themselves, made progress on their quilts. Sylvia made progress of her own, improving her patterns and teaching methods. She learned that good humor could make a difficult evaluation more tolerable, and that students were more likely to take her advice if she brought them around with encouragement instead of demanding they do what she knew was right. Her newfound wisdom came too late to help her when it would have done the most good for her personally, such as in countless childhood conflicts with her sister. It was too late to unsnarl the tangled threads of sibling antipathy now.

The quilting class continued, with mixed results. Mrs. Simmons dropped out of the group after Thanksgiving, but the others assured Sylvia that her decision had nothing to do with Sylvia's teaching. Sylvia believed them, but other students' offhand remarks suggested that they never intended to make another quilt after completing their first. To them, their expedition into quilting was a lark, not a pastime they were eager to pursue after this one enjoyable outing with friends. Most disheartening of all, the class was evenly divided between those who considered quilting to be an art form and those who considered it to be merely an enjoyable hobby.

Sylvia tried to persuade them that a quilt could be just as much a work of art as a painting or a sculpture. One woman finally relented, saying, "Perhaps quilts are art, dear — folk art." The other ladies were satisfied to see the debate end with that, but Sylvia thought it was a grudging compromise on their part, a nice, safe label that put quilting in a quaint little box but that ignored its true value. When she protested that on the day they first met at Mrs. Cass's house, they had admired her ancestor's masterpiece and declared it a true work of art, they considered her point briefly before concluding that antique quilts made generations ago could be called art, but that none of the quilts made in their day and age deserved that approbation.

Sylvia gave up in frustration. Even if only half of her class believed quilting was an art, that was six more people who believed it than before the class began. She would have to be content with that.

Christmas approached, and because the ladies of the Baltimore Quilting Circle were busy with holiday preparations and family gatherings, they agreed not to meet again until after the New Year.

Sylvia braced herself for the approaching holidays. Memories of Christmas mornings and hopeful New Year's Days at Elm Creek Manor filled her thoughts as she helped Mrs. Compson prepare the household for a bittersweet observation of the season. Mary and her husband were coming in from Washington, and with James's brothers and their sweethearts, as well as cousins and aunts and uncles from the city, the farmhouse would be full to the rafters with relatives by marriage Sylvia scarcely knew. James's absence from the family circle would be conspicuous.

As they baked Christmas cookies and pies, Mrs. Compson told stories of holidays when her children were young. Sylvia was both amused and pained to hear her tales of

James as a young boy. She craved any memory of her husband's life, even those that did not belong to her, because she would not be able to make new memories of life with him. And yet each story tore at her heart because that little boy and the good, loving man he had become were gone.

She remembered their first Christmas together as husband and wife, when in accordance with Bergstrom family tradition as the most recently married couple they had ventured out into the snowy woods to find the family Christmas tree. She thought back upon another, lonelier holiday when the men were at war, and she, Claudia, and Agnes had found strength and courage in their love for one another and in the simple joy and hope of the season. Those feelings should have sustained them when tragedy struck, but Claudia had betrayed them and Sylvia could never face her again.

When the time came to decorate the farmhouse at Compson's Resolution, Mrs. Compson sent her husband and sons into the wooded hills to bring home six small fir trees. Sylvia was jolted by a sudden memory of walking in the woods with James. They towed the bobsled behind them, James carried the ax, and he smiled as he told her about boyhood Christmases at his parents' house. "My father always wanted a floor-to-ceiling tree," he told her, "but my mother preferred a small one to stand on a tabletop. She said that was the way her family had always done it, and to please her, my father went along with it. Over the years they collected too many ornaments to fit on one small tree, but instead of getting a larger one, they chose two small trees and kept them in different rooms. By the time I was in school, we had small trees on tabletops in almost every room of the house. When visitors came, my sister and I would lead tours to make sure they didn't miss any of them."

Sylvia had smiled then, entranced by the image of her beloved husband as a boy on Christmas morning. Now the memory of his voice in the snowy woods made her ache with grief and longing.

Christmas Day came, a day she expected to be unable to endure, but although the family had not forgotten their sorrow, they found happiness in one another and in hope for the future. The war was over and more prosperous times seemed on the horizon. Mary's child was due within a month. Although Sylvia missed Elm Creek Manor more that day than she had since her departure, the love and acceptance the Compson family offered her helped her to feel the simple hope and joy of the season anew. She felt James's presence in the midst of his family, and she knew that his love for her remained, and that one day she would know love again.

The feeling of enduring love lingered until three days after Christmas, when Mrs. Compson approached Sylvia hesitantly, a letter in her hand. Sylvia knew at once who had sent it.

"Claudia heard from your Aunt Millie and Uncle George that you bought a train ticket to Baltimore," Mrs. Compson told her, when Sylvia refused to take the letter, which was addressed to her in-laws. "She asks if you're here with us, or if we know your whereabouts."

"Don't tell her I'm here."

"I have to tell her something," Mrs. Compson pointed out. "She'll think her letter went astray and send another, or she'll come to us herself."

Sylvia felt faint as a vision of a resentful Claudia at the farmhouse door crowded out her anger. "Tell her I stayed with you for a month, and left without telling you where I was going."

"You're asking me to lie?"

"Yes, I am."

"She sounds worried."

"She probably wants to gloat about her beautiful wedding." Claudia and Harold were the most recently married couple in the family now. They would have brought home the family Christmas tree that season as Sylvia and James had done, but there were few Bergstroms left at Elm Creek Manor to enjoy it. "She no doubt also wants to scold me for not attending. Does she offer anything in the way of an apology?"

Mrs. Compson scanned the letter. "No," she said, reluctantly, "but the letter is addressed to me and Charles. She didn't know you would be here to read it. If she had known, I'm sure she would have said how sorry she is that you two had a falling out."

"It was much more than a falling out, and I'm equally sure that she would not have apologized."

"You'll never know unless you return home."

The thought of wandering through Elm Creek Manor, hearing the voices of her lost loved ones whispering in the empty halls, catching glimpses of them in the corner of her eye, made Sylvia recoil in pain. "I can't."

Mrs. Compson regarded her for a long moment in silence before returning the letter to the envelope. "Very well. I'll do as you ask, but I hope someday soon you'll see how you've set up an insurmountable hurdle for your sister."

"What do you mean?"

"You want her to apologize, and yet you refuse to read her letter or go see her. How can she apologize if you won't listen? How can she ask for forgiveness if she can't find you?"

"I know my sister," said Sylvia. "She's never apologized to me for anything, not once in her life. She isn't about to start now."

Mrs. Compson tapped the envelope against the palm of her hand. "Why is she searching for you, then?"

Sylvia could not answer.

Mrs. Compson sighed. "Sylvia, dear, Charles and I are very happy to have you here with us, but eventually you're going to have to move on with your life. I believe your place is at Elm Creek Manor, but if you don't feel you can go home under these circumstances — well, only you can make that choice. But you must choose something. You can't continue to go through the motions of living. You have to truly live. You're still a young woman. You could marry again, have children —"

"No," said Sylvia. "I could never love

247

anyone else the way I loved James."

"Perhaps not," admitted Mrs. Compson. "But I know one thing for certain: James loved you. Don't choose a life of endless grieving for his sake. You are not honoring his memory by harboring anger in your heart. That is not what my son would have wanted for you."

Sylvia's gaze fell, unable to bear the weight of Mrs. Compson's compassion. She knotted her fingers together in her lap, her throat tightening. "I'm not ready to face my sister," she choked out. "I can't see her with Harold, not yet, not without hating her."

Mrs. Compson clasped Sylvia's hands in her own. "Think of the name of this farm, Compson's Resolution," she said. "A resolution is also the settlement of a dispute. Perhaps, with the New Year approaching, you will find the strength to make a resolution that will allow you to go home."

Sylvia closed her eyes against tears. She could not bear the thought of leaving the Compson farm. She felt safe here, hidden away, protected. But if Claudia suspected Sylvia was living on the farm, it could not shelter her forever.

New Year's Eve came. The Compson family stayed up until midnight reminiscing about bygone years and making hopeful predictions about the year ahead. Sylvia tried not to think about how Claudia, Harold, and Agnes were marking the holiday back home in Pennsylvania.

At midnight, to the strains of "Auld Lang Syne" on the radio broadcast of the Lombardo New Year's Eve Party, Sylvia and the Compsons toasted the New Year. "May the New Year bring us peace, contentment, and hope," said Mrs. Compson, raising her glass. "May each of us find the courage we need to overcome our sorrows and achieve the happiness we deserve."

Sylvia's eyes met hers over the rim of her glass, and she knew Mrs. Compson's wish was meant especially for her.

The next morning, Sylvia helped Mrs. Compson prepare breakfast for the family, missing Great-Aunt Lucinda's *Pfannkuchen.* She thought ruefully of the battered cookbook in the kitchen back home, stuffed full of recipes jotted down on index cards and the backs of envelopes in the handwriting of generations of Bergstrom women. She wished she had thought to take it with her when she fled Elm Creek Manor, even though the best family recipes would not be found there for they had never been written down. She longed for the aromas of pork roasting with apples, of sauerkraut, of her father's *Feuerzangenbowle.* It hardly felt like the New Year had begun without them.

She found herself telling her mother-in-law about all the old Bergstrom traditions, about lead pouring and unreliable predictions, of blazing fireballs and unfulfilled dreams. Mrs. Compson listened, almost forgetting the sausages frying on the stove. "And what about your dreams?" she asked when Sylvia finished. "Surely you must have a few left that you can still fulfill."

"I do." Sylvia had given her dreams a great deal of thought since Claudia's letter arrived. And after Mrs. Compson's New Year's Eve toast, she had determined to do something about them.

As the Compson sisters and brothers, cousins and uncles exchanged New Year's Day greetings, Sylvia thought of the generations past who had sat at that heirloom trestle table, glad to put the sorrows of the past year behind them, facing the year ahead with courage or with trepidation. Her story was a part of their history now, and although she would always long for James and for home, she found hope in knowing that for all that she had lost, she had also gained a second family. No matter where the year ahead took her, she would never truly be alone as long as she kept the memory of those she loved and those who loved her alive in her heart.

The conversation turned to New Year's resolutions. One aunt resolved to respond more promptly to friends' letters. James's sister, due to deliver her first baby any day, resolved to regain her slim figure by spring, which earned her a round of laughter from other mothers around the table.

"What about you, Sylvia?" prompted Mr. Compson. "Do you have any resolutions for the New Year?"

All eyes turned to her. Sylvia could imagine what the more distant relations saw when they looked at her: a poor curiosity, a fragile young widow overwhelmed by grief, inexplicably in flight from her family and the home she had always loved. Though they would never say anything to suggest she was not welcome among them, they probably wondered why she did not simply go home.

"I've made one resolution," Sylvia said. This was not how she had planned to tell them, but she plunged ahead. "I've decided to return to college."

An exclamation of surprise and delight went up from those gathered around the table. "Why, Sylvia, that's a wonderful idea," said Mrs. Compson. She knew that

Sylvia had left school after two years at Waterford College to marry James. "I'm sure a business degree will help you run Bergstrom Thoroughbreds."

"Perhaps I should be worried about the competition," remarked Mr. Compson, but he looked pleased.

"I'm not seeking a business degree," said Sylvia. "I want to become an art teacher." When Mrs. Compson's smile faded into confusion, Sylvia quickly added, "I've enjoyed teaching the Baltimore Quilting Circle ladies how to quilt, and I think I've discovered that I have a talent for teaching. I also want to show people how quiltmaking is a true art form. The more I learn about art, the more I'll be able to make that argument and back it up with critical thinking."

"Then —" Mr. Compson cleared his throat. "Then you have no intention of returning to Bergstrom Thoroughbreds?"

Sylvia laughed shakily. "I don't think a horse farm has much need for an art teacher on staff."

Some of the family members who did not know the story of Sylvia's self-imposed exile laughed, but James's parents and siblings looked stricken. "You do intend to resume your studies at Waterford College, though, don't you?" asked Mrs. Compson, her joy of moments ago all but vanished.

Sylvia had no intention of returning to the Elm Creek Valley, but she could not bear to admit to it and ruin her mother-in-law's New Year's Day. "I haven't thought that far ahead. I don't know if Waterford College would take me back after so many years, and I don't know if my credits would transfer if I were accepted somewhere else. Perhaps . . . perhaps I shouldn't have made a resolution without looking into it first."

Several people quickly assured her that her resolution was quite all right; she had set a goal for herself and that was the important thing. The rest could be sorted out later. Sylvia thanked them, but as the conversation moved on to others' resolutions, she glanced at Mrs. Compson and saw her exchange a look of dismay with her husband. When Sylvia had announced her resolution, Mrs. Compson had surely assumed that Sylvia would be returning to Elm Creek Manor and attending Waterford College only a few miles away. As much as Mrs. Compson wanted Sylvia to find the courage to fulfill her dreams, she would prefer for those dreams to set her on the road toward home.

Sylvia stayed on at Compson's Resolution while she planned her future. Winter ended and spring came to the farm. On Sylvia's birthday, Claudia sent another letter to the Compsons asking if they had heard from her. With a disapproving frown for her daughter-in-law, Mrs. Compson penned the reply Sylvia implored her to make: They were unaware of Sylvia's whereabouts, but if Sylvia contacted them, they would urge her to get in touch with Claudia. "That much is true," grumbled Mrs. Compson as she sealed the envelope. Not a week passed that she did not beg Sylvia to write to her sister.

A few days after the anniversary of James's death, the Compsons received an unexpected letter from Andrew. From his new home in Michigan, he wrote that he had been thinking of them and that he hoped they had friends and family nearby to see them through that difficult day. He shared memories of his friendship with James, of James's courage on the battlefield, of his reassuring confidence, his humor that helped them forget where they were, if only for moments. James had spoken of his family and Compson's Resolution often, Andrew wrote, and his descriptions of his boyhood home were so vivid that Andrew almost felt as if he had walked the wooded trails himself. "I know he loved you and Sylvia very much," he wrote. "He spoke of you often and he was looking forward to seeing you again. I want you to know that he saved my life more than once, and if I can live my life with half the courage, honor, and decency he demonstrated every day, I will consider myself a successful man."

Sylvia was in tears by the end of the letter. She wondered if Andrew had sent a similar letter to her at Elm Creek Manor. He would not know that she was not there to receive it.

By the end of summer, Sylvia had made her decision and could no longer conceal it from Mr. and Mrs. Compson. For months they had observed her preparing applications and checking the mail for information from prospective colleges. When the time came to break the news, however, she was unprepared for the depths of their disappointment. Upon hearing that she intended to enroll at Carnegie Mellon, Mrs. Compson became uncharacteristically tearful. "If Waterford College is out of the question, why not attend the University of Maryland?" she implored. "Mary received a wonderful education there, and you'd be close enough to come home for visits now and then. I know you applied; I know you were accepted. I've seen the postmarks."

Sylvia was touched by Mrs. Compson's heartfelt plea, especially because she had instinctively referred to Compson's Resolution and not Elm Creek Manor as Sylvia's home. But Carnegie Mellon suited her interests best, and a lingering fear remained that if she stayed too close to the Compsons, eventually Claudia would come looking for her.

On the morning she departed for Pittsburgh, she embraced her in-laws and thanked them for taking her into their home. "You're James's wife," her father-in-law said. "You'll always have a place here with us."

Sylvia promised to come visit them often, and she did, at first. On school holidays and summer vacations, she took the train east to Baltimore, gazing out the windows as they chugged south of the mountains surrounding the Elm Creek Valley, pressing her hand against the cool glass and longing for a glimpse of the land beyond the mountain passes.

After Sylvia graduated and began teaching in the Allegheny Valley School District, her visits to Compson's Resolution became less frequent. Mrs. Compson honored her promise not to disclose her whereabouts to Claudia, and eventually Claudia's letters stopped coming.

Whatever word the Compsons received of Elm Creek Manor or Bergstrom Thoroughbreds, they passed along to Sylvia. There were glad tidings for Agnes, Sylvia's former sister-in-law, for she had married a history professor from Waterford College. Darker rumors swirled that Bergstrom Thoroughbreds was failing, but Sylvia could not believe that even Claudia and Harold would allow the family business to falter so completely and so suddenly. Over time, news from Elm Creek Manor slowed to a trickle, and with Mr. and Mrs. Compson's passing, it stopped altogether.

As she grew older, Sylvia built lasting friendships with fellow quilters and neighbors near her red brick house on Camp Meeting Road in Sewickley, Pennsylvania. She offered her love for quilting to anyone who wanted to learn, and she was passionate about quilting as a traditional art form even before the "quilting renaissance" began in the 1970s. On every New Year's Eve, whether she celebrated alone or with friends, Sylvia reflected upon her mother-in-law's toast at Compson's Resolution. Had Sylvia found peace, contentment, and hope at long last, so far from home? Had she found the courage to overcome her sorrows and seek happiness?

Sylvia thought that she had. This was not the life she had expected, but it was rewarding, and she was thankful.

Fifty years after leaving Elm Creek Manor, she received a phone call from a lawyer, the son of a man she had known as a classmate in Waterford. She was stunned when he told her Claudia had died. "How?" she stammered, shaken. Of course Claudia had aged as she herself had aged, although in her mind's eye Claudia had been frozen in time exactly as she had been in 1945. People their age died every day, and others called it natural causes.

Harold had preceded Claudia in death and they had no children, so the estate was Sylvia's. She was not sure she wanted it. She had made a life for herself in Sewickley, and she could not imagine rattling around the manor alone, not at her age, not when none of her friends remained nearby. She hired a private detective to find a more suitable heir — a distant relation, anyone. When the quest proved fruitless — so promptly that Sylvia wondered if the detective had searched as thoroughly as his fees merited — Sylvia returned to Elm Creek Manor as the sole heir of the Bergstrom estate.

It was late September when she made the trip through the rolling hills of central Pennsylvania to the Elm Creek Valley. She almost could not breathe as she turned off the main highway onto the narrow, gravel road that led through a wood encircling the Bergstrom property, ablaze with the hues of autumn. Her heart was in her throat as the taxi rambled over the old stone bridge crossing Elm Creek, curious, but fearing what she would see upon emerging from the woods. The broad, dry front lawn was overgrown, but the gray stone walls of the manor stood proudly above it. The Bergstrom legacy seemed as strong and resilient as ever until the cab pulled to a stop in the circular driveway and Sylvia beheld peeling paint, broken windowpanes, and crumbling mortar.

The lawyer's warnings had not adequately prepared her for what she discovered inside. Claudia had sold off many family heirlooms to make ends meet after the business failed, but the empty spaces once occupied by valuable antique furniture and fine art startled her at every turn. As if to make up for ridding the manor of its treasures, Claudia had stuffed rooms full of worthless clutter — junk mail, yellowing newspapers, meat trays from the supermarket, burned out light bulbs, quart jars that had once held spaghetti sauce. Sylvia could not fathom why her sister had hoarded so much useless rubbish. What had she intended to do with it all? How many empty mason jars did one woman need, especially a woman who had let the garden run wild and had nothing to can? Was it nothing more than one last spiteful jab at her estranged sister, whom Claudia must have suspected would be responsible for cleaning up the mess?

Sylvia tackled the kitchen first, but hours of labor made little headway. Exhausted, she made up a bed on the sofa in the west sitting room, for the thought of spending the night in the room she and James had once shared was unbearable. When she woke the next morning in the empty house, she felt pinned to the bed by the sheer weight of the enormous task awaiting her. The manor was hers, now, as well as the remaining lands that Claudia had failed to or forgotten to sell off. She had to meet with the lawyer and pay her sister's debts. Every room had to be cleared, the rubbish sorted from items worth keeping. There were details and entanglements to sort out, papers to sign, accounts to close. It would take her at least a month, and she had packed for only a few days. She would have to make a trip into Waterford for groceries and pray that the old stove and icebox still worked.

Waterford had changed since she had seen it last — progress, she supposed some people would call it — and it seemed both familiar and strange. The college had expanded; a few buildings downtown had been demolished and replaced. There was a new quilt shop on Main Street, so she stopped in to browse for a while and chatted with the friendly owner. At least if she was forced to extend her stay, she needn't fear running out of quilting supplies.

Spending a solitary Christmas at Elm Creek Manor was out of the question. Bygone seasons of warmth and laughter now seemed shrouded in perpetual mourning. Every room, every possession reminded her of faces she would never see again, voices she would never hear. She closed up the old house and returned to Sewickley to spend the holiday in the company of friends. As dear as they were to her, they knew little of her past before she came to Sewickley as a young widow. Some believed she had lived all her life in Sewickley and were surprised to learn of a long-lost sister and family estate in the Elm Creek Valley. They offered condolences for her loss and assistance in tying up the loose ends of Claudia's estate, but Sylvia knew the task was hers alone — and a more arduous task than they suspected. Not wanting to boast, she had not been completely honest about the size of the estate or its former elegance. She certainly hadn't referred to it as a "manor."

"You won't be leaving us for your old family home in the country, will you, Sylvia?" asked one friend, half in worry, half in jest.

"There's little chance of that," said Sylvia. "I left home fifty years ago. Nothing remains for me there."

Later, another friend took Sylvia aside and urged her not to make any hasty decisions. "When my husband died last year, I couldn't bear to see any of his things," Alice confided. "I told my sons to take anything they wanted, and I gave everything else to Goodwill. I saved only photographs, his war medals, and his wedding ring. Now my house is clean and tidy, and there are days when I miss him so much I want nothing more than to slip into one of his old flannel shirts and read a book by the fire and pretend he's there with me. And I can't."

"Oh, Alice." Sylvia embraced her. "I'm so sorry."

"Who would have thought that what I'd miss most would turn out to be his favorite flannel shirt?" said Alice wistfully. "If I had waited another month for the weather to turn colder, I'm sure I would have known. Sylvia, I understand you can't sit on that old place forever, especially since it's so far away, but please don't make my mistake. Don't get rid of everything until you've had time to carefully reflect upon what it might mean to you later. I can guess that you and your sister didn't get along, but there must be a few mementos you'd like to keep. If not your sister's belongings, then perhaps your parents'." Alice pressed her arm. "There's no rush. Promise yourself you won't do anything you can't undo."

Sylvia thanked Alice for her wise advice and promised to take heed.

Two days after Christmas, she returned to Elm Creek Manor with a renewed sense of purpose. The details of Claudia's estate were nearly resolved, and a decision loomed before her. As she deliberated over the fate of the manor, she chose a precious few family keepsakes to treasure always. Her friends assumed she would follow the most sensible course — sell the property and return to Sewickley. Still, Sylvia had been away from the manor so long that she didn't care to hasten her final leavetaking. It troubled her, too, to think of selling the estate to a stranger when it had belonged to the Berg-stroms since the day Hans, Anneke, and Gerda Bergstrom had set the cornerstone in place.

In the kitchen she discovered her Great-Aunt Lucinda's cookie cutters. She set those aside in the west sitting room, along with photograph albums and her father's watch. She wanted one of her mother's quilts, perhaps her New York Beauty wedding quilt or the Elms and Lilacs anniversary quilt, but she did not find either spread on any of the beds. They were such exquisite quilts that very likely they had been put away for safekeeping, so she decided to continue her search for them later. To her surprise she found a Featherweight sewing machine in the parlor; Agnes or Claudia must have purchased it after Sylvia's departure.

Suddenly Sylvia remembered Great-Grandmother Anneke's sewing machine in the west sitting room. Sylvia spent part of every day there, and it was strange she had not thought of it before. When she reached the doorway, she understood why: It had been pushed into the corner away from its customary spot and draped with a graying bedsheet.

"Customary spot," Sylvia said with a derisive sniff. More than fifty years had passed since she had known what was "customary" around Elm Creek Manor.

She tugged off the sheet and sneezed as a cloud of dust encircled her. Waving the motes away, Sylvia blinked her watering eyes and sighed with relief at the sight of the priceless treadle sewing machine Anneke had brought with her to America. Family stories handed down through the generations claimed that she had helped support the family by taking in sewing from a dressmaker in town. Her skills with a needle and thread were as legendary as Gerda's reputation as a cook.

Then Sylvia peered closer. Wedged between the foot pedal and the sewing machine cabinet were two overstuffed laundry bags. Curious, Sylvia carefully extricated them from their hiding spot and untied the drawstrings of one of the bags. Inside, she discovered the Bergstrom women's scrap collection, as well as folded yardage of more recent acquisitions.

Sylvia settled down on the floor, her heart pounding with anticipation. Gazing into the bag, she quickly recognized strips of bright calico her Great-Aunt Lucinda had cut for cousin Elizabeth's Chimneys and Cornerstones quilt. She found pretty florals from which she and Claudia had carefully cut squares for the Nine-Patch quilt they had sewn for a newborn cousin. Pastel scraps left over from her mother's Elms and Lilacs anniversary quilt mingled with red patches from Agnes's failed attempt to make a Double Wedding Ring quilt for Richard. Fabrics familiar and unknown kept a jumbled account of landmark moments in the Bergstrom women's lives, occasions they had marked with the creation of a quilt. Births and celebrations, times of learning and times of teaching others — Sylvia could find a memento of each within the soft cotton scraps so long forgotten.

Blue and yellow had always been her lucky colors. As if she could feel the Bergstrom women gathering nearby, urging her on, Sylvia searched through the bags and withdrew all the blue and yellow-gold scraps she could find.

It was New Year's Eve, the time for reflection. As Sylvia cut fabric and traced templates, she thought back upon all the New Year's Eves she had spent sheltered within the gray stone walls of the manor and within the even stronger circle of love of her family. As she sewed a Good Fortune block into the center of a Mother's Favorite pattern, memories of decades of New Years greeted far from home cast melancholy shadows upon the seasons past, but she did not flinch. If she were to take an honest look at her life and her choices, she could not pick and choose what to remember. The New Year had not always fulfilled its promise of good fortune, and when it had not, it had been up to her to make the most of what was given, to learn and to grow, and in so doing, to turn ill fortune into good. In the stillness of her heart, she knew she had sometimes stumbled along the way, had allowed fear or anger or resentment to prevent her from living as fully as she could have. She could not change the mistakes of the past, but she could learn from them.

Sylvia worked on her New Year's Reflections quilt, adding a Peace and Plenty block in tribute to Josephine Compson and the New Year's blessing she had bestowed upon her family so many years before. She pieced a Memory Chain block so she would never forget the hard lessons learned from the unexpected course her life had taken. She sewed, lost in thought, until the clock struck midnight. There were no noisemakers, no champagne toasts, no kisses and cries of "Happy New Year" ringing through the halls, but this New Year's Day would mark a new beginning for Sylvia, for she had resolved what course to pursue in the year ahead.

She would clear the manor of Claudia's detritus, bringing in a forklift if necessary. She would hire workers to make repairs and get the grounds in decent shape. Then, when the manor was no longer an embarrassment to the Bergstrom name, she would sell it and return to her home and friends in Sewickley.

For as much as she wanted to blame her sister for the manor's disrepair, she knew that she was at least as much at fault. She had abandoned home, family, and business, knowing that Claudia and Harold were not fit stewards of the Bergstrom legacy. What had befallen Elm Creek Manor was as much her responsibility as Claudia's, perhaps more.

Sylvia resolved that although she would sell the manor, she would not entrust the Bergstrom estate to just anyone. As long as it took, she would wait for a buyer who would restore the manor to its former glory, who would fill the halls with love and laughter once more. She had no idea who could possibly fit the bill, but she would wait until that person came along. She had mishandled the Bergstrom legacy once, but she would not fail her family a second time.

As long as she lived, the New Year's Reflections quilt would remind her of her resolution.

As Sylvia made small, neat stitches to secure the binding to the back of the quilt, she smiled when she thought of the resolution she had made in the first minutes of that New Year and the unexpected way she had kept it.

The following summer, she had hired a young woman named Sarah McClure to help her clean out the manor and prepare it for sale. One prospective buyer had spoken of turning the manor into a residence hall for students of Waterford College, and Sylvia had been tempted to accept his offer. No one else with a more attractive plan had appeared in all the months the estate had been on the market, and as a retired teacher, Sylvia liked the idea of offering students such a beautiful place to live. To Sylvia's everlasting gratitude, Sarah became suspicious of the developer's plans and secretly investigated his company. When Sarah learned that the developer intended to raze Elm Creek Manor and build condos on the property, Sylvia immediately broke off negotiations. At a loss for what to do next, she asked Sarah to help her find a way to bring the manor back to life. Sarah's ingenious and unlikely suggestion was to turn Elm Creek Manor into a retreat for quilters, a place for them to stay, to learn, to find inspiration, and to enjoy the companionship of other quilters. The new owners she had resolved to find turned out to be herself, Sarah, and a group of local quilters who became the first staff members of Elm Creek Quilt Camp.

Thank heavens Sylvia had accepted Sarah's proposal, or her beloved home would now be rubble in a demolition landfill. What a blessing it was that Elm Creek Quilts had prospered, or Sylvia might have been forced to sell the manor anyway, and she would have been a hundred miles distant when Andrew pulled up in his motor home for the surprise visit of a lifetime. She had thought he had forgotten her long ago, and she had been delighted to resume their friendship. She never would have guessed that their feelings would grow deeper and that they would fall in love.

The New Year's wish Mrs. Compson had made for her so many years ago had come true at last.

As they drove through Hartford, Sylvia smiled up at Andrew, her heart full of joy and affection. "I'm so glad you came back to Elm Creek Manor," she told him. "I'm thankful I was there when you came."

"Not half as thankful as I am," he said.

She realized, then, that no matter what Amy decided, whether she chose the wise course of reconciliation or resolved to close her heart to her father, Sylvia and Andrew would be all right. Their love and their gratitude for the blessing of that love would help them endure whatever difficulties came their way.

They turned onto a broad, tree-lined street, recently cleared after what must have been a heavy snowfall. A few houses sported snowmen in the front yards, others impressive snow forts where children in snowsuits and mittens pelted one another with snowballs.

Andrew pulled into the driveway of a sage-green Victorian home with a broad front porch and an octagonal turret on the southeast corner. Evergreen boughs wrapped with small, gold Christmas lights graced the front porch railing and a wreath of fresh holly adorned the front door.

He shut down the engine and paused with his hand on the keys as if tempted to start the car and tear back down the driveway. But Andrew never lacked for courage, so instead he pocketed the keys and gave Sylvia what he probably thought was an encouraging grin. "We're here."

Sylvia was seized by a sudden fear. "Please tell me they're expecting us."

"I called from the 1863 House," he assured her, peering up at the house's darkened windows. Small, icy crystals of snow fell upon the windshield, gently threatening to obscure the view. "But . . . that doesn't mean they're here."

"Perhaps they left town when they heard we were on our way."

Andrew snorted, but the question was promptly settled when the front door opened and Amy stepped out on the front porch, unsmiling, folding her arms over her chest against the cold.

CHAPTER FIVE

Amy disappeared into the house but returned to the porch dressed in a coat and boots just as Andrew and Sylvia finished unloading their suitcases from the Elm Creek Quilts minivan. "Here, Dad, let me help you with that," Amy said, hurrying down the front steps.

"I think I can handle two suitcases," said Andrew.

Sylvia had to fight the urge to roll her eyes. Already it had begun. "If she wants to help, let her," she murmured, but Andrew pretended not to hear. He carried both suitcases into the house, with Amy and Sylvia trailing after.

Daniel and the three lanky teenagers — grandsons Gus and Sam, granddaughter Caitlin — welcomed them in the foyer with warm hugs and cheerful smiles. Only Amy seemed ill at ease. The grandchildren, thankfully, seemed unaware of any conflict between the adults, which Sylvia took as a hopeful sign.

"I have pot roast in the oven," Amy announced, taking their coats and hanging them on a mahogany coat tree in a corner near the door. "It'll be ready in a half hour, so please, come on inside and make yourselves at home."

It was certainly a much warmer welcome than Sylvia had anticipated. She prayed that Andrew would not spoil it by blurting out a wedding announcement.

Amy led them into the living room and offered them hot beverages. Sylvia gladly accepted a cup of peppermint tea and settled down on the comfortable sofa. In the fireplace, blazing pine logs crackled cheerfully and gave off steady warmth. In front of the picture window stood a stately Norway pine, festooned with small white lights. Blown glass figurines hung amidst glittering silver tinsel, candy canes, and ornaments the children must have made in school many years before. Every fragrant bough offered a glimpse of a family as it grew and changed, from the crystal swans engraved with the year Amy and Daniel married, to the gilt frames bearing school photographs, to keepsake ornaments revealing the children's favorite sports and cartoon characters. Sylvia's gaze fell upon a pair of delicate white snowflakes, embroidered with pale blue silk threads and as intricate as lace. "How lovely."

"My mother made those," said Amy. "She didn't have much time for crafts, but she loved Hardanger embroidery. One year when Bob and I were still in elementary school, the women of the neighborhood had a Christmas ornament exchange party. My mom made dozens of these, and I begged her to let me have these two. She was surprised that I wanted them but I think she was flattered, too. I've placed them on my Christmas tree every year since." She gazed at the feathery snowflakes and smiled wistfully. "I miss her so much at this time of year. The holidays just aren't the same without her."

Andrew put his arm around her and she briefly rested her head on his shoulder. Sylvia's heart lightened as she witnessed the silent exchange between father and daughter. Despite their recent disagreements, they surely loved each other too much to allow Andrew's remarriage to divide them forever. If Amy's pride and Andrew's stubbornness did not get in the way, surely they would choose reconciliation over estrangement.

When supper was ready, the family gathered in the dining room, where a centerpiece of candles and poinsettias gave the antique cherry dining table a festive air. The roast and potatoes made for a hearty meal, perfect for a snowy winter evening. Sylvia found it encouraging that although Amy had set out the good china, she had chosen a homey, comforting meal one would serve at a gathering of friends and family rather than a stuffy, formal menu meant to impress a not-entirely-welcome guest. Two hours into the visit, all was going well — so well that Sylvia wished she and Andrew had agreed to wait until the morning to make their announcement.

"Do you have any plans for New Year's Eve?" Sylvia asked. "Our family kept many German-American traditions that don't seem to be followed in the Old Country anymore. At our bed and breakfast in New York, we met a charming couple from Germany who told us that everyone in their country — and they did emphasize *everyone* — watches a particular television program that sounded a little unusual to me."

"New Year's Rockin' Eve from Berlin with David Hasselhoff?" guessed Gus.

Sylvia laughed and explained about *Dinner for One,* knowing that she was telling the story not only to amuse her listeners, but also to postpone their announcement. She wished she could have a moment alone with Andrew so she could ask him to wait, but perhaps it was just as well. It had been her idea, after all, to reveal the truth early in their visit. As much as she dreaded Amy's reaction, they ought to get it over with and hope for the best.

Andrew held off breaking the news until after supper. The grandchildren cleared the table as Amy brought out coffee, but before the youngsters could return to their video games and IM chat rooms, or whatever it was that so absorbed them on the computer, he asked them to take their seats again.

As the teenagers seated themselves, exchanging curious smiles, Amy grew very still at the foot of the table. Sylvia said a silent prayer for peace and wished for just a moment that Andrew had broken the news over the phone.

"What is it, Dad?" Amy asked. "You're not . . . ill, are you?"

"No, no," said Andrew. "I've never felt better, and part of the reason is that I am now the proud husband of this lovely woman right here."

With that, he laced his fingers through Sylvia's, smiled at her reassuringly, and raised her hand to his lips.

The grandchildren cheered, and Daniel smiled broadly. "Congratulations," he said, clapping his father-in-law on the back. He rose and came around to Sylvia to kiss her on the cheek.

Amy sat wide-eyed and still, her gaze fixed on her father. "You mean you're her *fiancé*," she said. "You said *husband*."

"I didn't misspeak," said Andrew. "Sylvia and I married on Christmas Eve."

Amy stared at him, slowly comprehending. "Are you trying to say that you eloped?"

"We had a lovely wedding at Elm Creek Manor," said Sylvia. "It's true that we caught most of our friends by surprise, but we don't consider that eloping."

"Not that anything's wrong with that," said Sam. "Congratulations, Grandpa. You want to play Xbox with us? We have four controllers." His older brother nudged him. "What? What did I say?"

Crushed, Caitlin wailed, "You mean we missed everything?"

"We wanted you to be there," Andrew said. His gaze shifted from Daniel to Amy. "You and Bob and Kathy and their kids and the whole family. Now you understand why we were so eager for you to come for Christmas."

"If we had known you were going to get

married, we would have made the trip," said Amy.

"Why, so you could stop us? You told us you couldn't come for Christmas, but we were supposed to know that you could suddenly become available if a wedding was involved?"

"Andrew, this isn't the way," murmured Sylvia.

"The wedding was a surprise," Daniel said to his wife. "They couldn't tell us or they'd spoil it."

"Why did it have to be a surprise?" said Amy, her voice rising. "Wasn't the engagement surprise enough? The wedding has to be a shock, too?"

"Let's all just take a deep breath and settle down," said Sylvia.

"Seriously, like, peace out, people," said Caitlin, folding her arms and shaking her head at her mother and grandfather.

Amy glared at her daughter. "I don't appreciate your tone, and was that even a sentence?"

Caitlin rolled her eyes.

"If you had really wanted us at your wedding, you would have told us," said Amy, turning to her father. "Do you think I'm stupid? I know what happened. You knew we didn't approve, so you invited us just so that you could say you tried, and then you snuck your wedding in under the radar."

"Would you have come if you had known?" said Andrew. "Would you have supported us, or would you have stood up and thrown a tantrum when the judge asked if anyone had any reason to object to the marriage? Maybe it's just as well that you didn't come."

Amy pushed her chair back from the table, but Sylvia quickly placed a hand on her arm. "Please stay. Let's work this out."

"What's to work out?" snapped Amy, but she stayed in her seat.

Sylvia clasped her hands together in her lap. "Perhaps we should have handled things better, and if we've offended you, I'm sincerely sorry. What's important now is that we are married, and we're hoping that you can find it in your heart to be happy for us. If happiness is out of the question at this particular moment — and I can understand why it might be — we ask instead for your acceptance."

Amy refused to look at her. "How can we offer you our acceptance when you gave us no say in the matter?"

"Because you don't deserve any say in the matter," said Andrew, incredulous. "It was never up to you whether I married, or whom, or when, or how. This was between Sylvia and me. It was never a group decision."

"Nothing around here is ever a group decision," muttered Caitlin.

"That's enough out of you, young lady," snapped Amy.

Caitlin sniffed in disdain, rose deliberately from her chair, and left the room. Her brothers exchanged quick, wary looks and decided to follow her example.

Daniel planted his elbows on the table and cradled his head in his hands. "Just for the record, I think you two make a great couple and I wish you both years of happiness."

"Daniel," gasped Amy.

"Oh, come on, honey, you know where I stand."

"Yes, against me, apparently."

"This isn't about you." Daniel gestured to the newlyweds. "It's about them. It's about their happiness. Sylvia's right. What's done is done. It's time for us to come together as a family."

"They're flaunting their wedding in my face and I'm supposed to act happy about it?"

"That would be better than acting like a spoiled brat," said Andrew.

In a gesture reminiscent of her daughter's,

Amy gave him a steady, wordless look before rising from her chair and striding from the room.

"I'm sorry," Daniel told the newlyweds.

"It's not your fault," Sylvia assured him as he hurried after his wife.

"I should have known this would happen," muttered Andrew when they were alone.

"It was bound to happen," said Sylvia. "You walked in here with a chip on your shoulder daring Amy to disapprove of us. Honestly, Andrew, you could have handled this much better."

"You're blaming me?"

"Oh, there's plenty of blame to go around." She reached for his hand. "We both knew she would take the news badly. If only you had responded with more compassion instead of losing your temper —"

"I know," said Andrew, chagrined. "I know. I should have behaved myself, but Sylvia, when she started in on you —"

"I've told you before, dear, it takes more than angry words to bring me to my knees." Sylvia shook her head. Everything had gone so wrong so quickly. "She's being unreasonable, you're overreacting, and I'm afraid we're much worse off than we were before."

Andrew frowned and rubbed at his jaw. "What do we do now?"

"I think there's only one thing we can do."

"What's that?"

"Give her what she's asked for."

Breakfast the next morning was a tense affair. Amy hardly spoke, and she was clearly just as angry with her husband as with Sylvia and her father. The grandkids tried to lighten the mood with jokes and amusing stories, but they grew discouraged when their listeners barely smiled. Caitlin persisted long after her brothers gave up, peppering Sylvia with questions about the wedding. Mindful of Amy who was studiously ignoring the conversation, Sylvia provided an understated description of the candlelight ceremony in the ballroom of the manor, restored to its former elegance thanks to the attention of Sarah McClure's husband, Matt, who had become the full-time gardener and caretaker of the estate.

"Have you told Bob and Kathy yet?" Daniel asked Andrew, referring to Andrew's son and daughter-in-law.

"Not yet," Andrew replied.

"Don't expect a shower of rose petals," said Amy shortly. "I doubt they'll welcome the news any more than we did. The girls wanted to be bridesmaids, as I'm sure you recall."

Andrew peered at her curiously. "Are you angry now because we got married or because we got married without you? I've lost track."

Sylvia frowned. Why must Andrew rise to the bait every time Amy spoke?

"I wanted to be a bridesmaid, too, but you don't see me whining," said Caitlin. "My cousins will get over it. The important thing is that you got married the way you wanted to."

"Not entirely the way we wanted," said Sylvia. "We wanted all of you to be there. Truly, we did."

Caitlin shrugged and made a face to suggest it didn't matter. "What should we call you now, anyway? Mrs. Cooper?"

"No, I've decided not to change my last name. I've been Sylvia Compson so long that I don't think I'd remember to answer to anything else."

"But it's not like you're keeping your maiden name," Amy pointed out. "You're actually keeping your first husband's name instead of taking my father's. Some people might think that suggests a lack of commitment."

Andrew loaded scrambled eggs onto a piece of buttered toast. "If it doesn't bother me, it shouldn't bother you."

Caitlin threw her mother a brief scowl before returning her attention to Sylvia. "Should we call you Grandma?"

Amy slammed her palm on the table. "She is not your grandmother."

"We can't call her 'Step-Grandma,' " said Sam. "That's so lame."

"Lame or not, like it or not, that's all she is."

Andrew glowered. "All right, now, I've had just about enough —"

"We've all had just about enough." Sylvia rose. "I can't bear to think that I've divided this family. Amy, you're right. You win." She turned to Andrew and steeled herself. "I'm sorry, dear. Our marriage was a mistake. When we return to Elm Creek Manor, I'm going to file for an annulment."

Andrew looked up at her, pain in his eyes. "Sylvia —"

Sylvia managed a tender smile, blinked back her tears, and hurried from the room.

Upstairs in the guest room, Sylvia rolled Andrew's suitcase into the hallway and shut the door. If she wasn't going to stay married to a man, she couldn't share a bedroom with him.

She arranged pillows into a comfortable seat on the bed and retrieved the New Year's Reflections quilt from her tote bag. She spread the quilt over her lap and gazed upon it, her heart momentarily lifted by the soothing colors and the intricate patterns. Threading a needle, she got to work, wondering if Amy would still be willing to accept her gift or if all her efforts had been in vain.

Through the closed door she heard the muffled sounds of heated debate as she mitered the last of the four corners. Voices rose and fell as she turned her attention to the last edge of the quilt. She couldn't hear the details of the argument, but she could imagine the way things were going. Five minutes of silence told her they had reached an impasse, and sure enough, before long she heard footsteps approaching from the far end of the hallway.

The door swung open and Andrew leaned inside. He gestured to the suitcase at his feet. "You're throwing me out?"

She raised her eyebrows at him over the rims of her glasses. "It wouldn't be proper to do otherwise."

Andrew frowned, but he could hardly disagree. "You're not going to stay locked up here until the New Year, are you?"

Sylvia considered. "As tempting as that might be, I don't think so. Now that Amy has had her own way, I imagine it will be much more pleasant downstairs now that we've made her so happy."

"Oh, you'll see how happy she is," Andrew said scornfully as Sylvia returned quilt and notions to her tote bag.

The grandkids had made themselves scarce, and Sylvia couldn't blame them. In the kitchen, Amy and Daniel were rinsing the breakfast dishes and loading the dishwasher. "May I help?" asked Sylvia.

"No," said Amy. "We've got it, thanks."

She did not look in Sylvia's direction, but it was obvious she had been crying. Sylvia pretended not to notice, sat down at the kitchen table, and idly paged through the newspaper.

Andrew pulled out a chair beside her. "Is there anything I can do to change your mind?"

"I'm afraid not, dear." Sylvia passed him the sports section, but he ignored it. "This is best for everyone."

"How can you say that?"

"With me out of the picture, you and your children can —" She waved a hand, searching for the appropriate phrase. "Go back to normal."

"As if nothing ever happened? That's not possible. I'll always remember that they were responsible for driving you away. It'll be impossible to forgive them. Our divorce would divide the family more than our marriage ever could."

Sylvia saw Amy and Daniel exchange an anxious look. "Perhaps this is a discussion better made in private," Sylvia said, lowering her voice a fraction. "We have a long drive home. We can save it for then."

Andrew threw up his hands in exasperation. "And when we get 'home,' what then?"

"Oh, dear. You're right. I hadn't thought of that."

Amy couldn't restrain her curiosity. "Thought of what?"

"I can't very well live with Sylvia after we divorce, can I?" said Andrew. "Elm Creek Manor has been my home for years, but not any more. Where am I supposed to go?"

"Didn't Bob and Kathy ask you to live with them?" Amy asked in a small voice.

"That's crazy talk. You know how small those southern California tract houses are. We'll be tripping over each other. And I sure can't sleep on their fold-out sofa for the rest of my life, not with my back."

"Well . . . there's your RV, for the immediate future. You can even park it at Elm Creek Manor through the winter, if you like. But —" Sylvia threw an imploring look to Amy and Daniel. "I don't think anyone would expect you to live in the RV forever."

"You can move in with us," said Daniel, placing an arm around his wife's shoulders. "It's the least we can do, since we're responsible for Sylvia's decision."

"Wait." Amy shrugged off her husband's arm and held up her hands. "Maybe we're being too hasty here."

"Do you have a VFW in town?" Andrew asked Daniel. "Can I park the RV in your driveway or would it be better on the street in front of the house?"

Sylvia beamed at Amy. "You're such a generous daughter, opening your home to your father, especially with the children going off to college in a few years. Taking on all that cooking and laundry and chauffeuring just when you were probably looking forward to more time to yourself — well, I don't think one daughter in ten would be so generous."

"I hope you didn't have any other plans for that guest room," said Andrew.

Amy shook her head, looking faintly ill. "I was thinking about turning it into a sewing room, but —"

"Oh, dear," exclaimed Sylvia. "I suppose we won't be able to continue your quilting lessons, since this will surely be my last visit."

"Can I redecorate?" asked Andrew. "No offense, but that room's awfully lacy and frilly. I'd like to hang up my fishing trophies."

"Dead trout on a varnished plank, that's what I always called them," Sylvia confided.

"Maybe the kids can drive me around town when you're too busy," Andrew mused. "They all have their licenses by now, right? I don't think I should take the RV around on errands unless you have very forgiving neighbors. These streets are so narrow I might knock over a few mailboxes."

Sylvia, Andrew, and Daniel all began talking at once, their voices a babble of redecorating suggestions and driving tips. In the center of it all, Amy clutched her head in her hands, her gaze flicking around the room as if desperate to find an escape.

Before long Amy had clearly heard enough. "All right, all right!" When the others fell silent, she closed her eyes and inhaled deeply. "Dad, Daniel, will you excuse Sylvia and me for a minute?"

"Why?" said Daniel, wary.

Amy looked as if another word might cause her to explode. "Just go. Please."

Daniel nudged his father-in-law and gestured toward the door. Andrew struggled to hide a grin as they left the kitchen. Sylvia knew he was thinking that this would be his moment of triumph. This was Amy's cue to beg Sylvia not to divorce him.

Sylvia wasn't so sure that was what Amy had in mind, but she pushed the newspaper aside and composed herself as Amy pulled up a chair on the other side of the table. "I take it you want to speak to me alone?"

"My father would just waste time proclaiming his innocence, but I doubt you will," said Amy. "You can let the curtain fall on the drama now. Please."

"I beg your pardon?"

"The breaking up with my father act. I know what you're doing, and I think I know why."

Sylvia sighed. "How did you know? Was our acting really that bad?"

"My father loves you," Amy said. "If he believed you really intended to divorce him, he wouldn't be talking about parking spaces for his RV and hanging dead fish on the walls. He would be brokenhearted. He would be devastated. And I think you would be, too."

Reluctantly, Sylvia admitted, "I suppose the lack of tears and pleading was a dead giveaway."

"And also, yes, your acting really was that bad."

"It couldn't have been," said Sylvia. "You were genuinely alarmed for a few minutes. I saw it in your eyes when visions of cleaning up after your father and losing your sewing room flashed before your eyes."

"I might have had a nervous moment or two."

"Your father hoped to drag this out for at least another day," said Sylvia. "He thought that given a taste of how his life and yours would be affected if we were no longer together, you'd give our marriage your heartiest endorsement."

Amy managed a small smile. "That's ridiculous."

"We had to try something. Reasoning with you wasn't working. Arguing made matters worse." Sylvia laced her fingers together and rested them on the table. "Frankly, Amy, I'm at a loss. You've said you're concerned because I had a stroke. My doctor and I agree that I've fully recovered and that I'm in excellent health, but even if you're right and we're wrong, I have sufficient resources that you needn't fear your father will exhaust himself caring for me."

"It's not just that. I'm thinking of the emotional toll if he loses you. You didn't see what he went through, tending my mother in her last years, mourning her when she died."

"Your father already loves me, so if I do pass on before he does, he will mourn me whether I'm his friend or his wife. I could lose him. You could lose Daniel. That can't stop us from loving." Sylvia shook her head, knowing nothing she said would persuade Amy to see reason. "We've told you all this before, dear, and not once have you disagreed. You accept our premises but not our conclusions, so I can't help thinking there's something else behind your disapproval."

Amy studied her for a long moment in silence. "There is."

"I thought so." Sylvia reached for her hand. "Amy, dear, you're not betraying your mother's memory by accepting my marriage to your father."

Amy said nothing, but her eyes filled with unshed tears.

"I could never replace your mother," said Sylvia. "I would never try. Your father found love a second time. That doesn't mean he's forgotten your mother or that his love for her wasn't strong and true."

"He knew you first," Amy choked out, snatching her hand away. "But you were married to another man. Was that the only reason he married my mother? Was she his second choice, and all these long years he was putting on an act, pining away for you?"

Aghast, Sylvia sat back in her chair. "Amy —"

"If that's true, then everything I ever learned about love since I was a child has been a lie."

"Oh, Amy, you couldn't be more wrong." Sylvia hardly knew where to begin. "What has your father told you about his time in the service?"

"Very little," said Amy with a bitter laugh. "You know what men of his generation are like. They don't complain; they don't brag. They just do what needs to be done — whether that's winning a war or keeping a marriage vow even when your heart longs to be with someone else."

Sylvia silently promised herself to prevail upon Andrew to clear away Amy's misunderstandings. She deserved to know what a fine man he was, even if that forced him to boast. "There's so much to say and it's your father's place to say it," she said. "For now, you need to know that your mother was indeed your father's first choice. She always was his true love."

"We'll never know for sure."

"On the contrary, we do know," said Sylvia. "My husband was killed during the war.

When your father came home after his service ended, he came to see me at Elm Creek Manor. If he had wanted to declare his love for me, he had the perfect opportunity."

"He wouldn't have considered that an appropriate time," said Amy, with such certainty that Sylvia decided that perhaps she knew her father well after all. "You had just lost your husband. He wouldn't have made a move on a grieving widow."

"Perhaps not," said Sylvia, amused in spite of everything at the thought of the gentlemanly Andrew "making a move" on anyone. "But he surely would have stayed nearby, so that when the time was right, he would be in the right place. Instead he took a job hundreds of miles away where he met your mother and fell in love." Sylvia forced herself to confess her own guilty secret. "There are days, I admit, when I wish he had been in love with me back then, and that he had stayed in Waterford, courted me, and asked me to marry him while we were still young. If he had, I would have been spared years of loneliness. I almost certainly would have remained at Elm Creek Manor. I could have reconciled with my sister, kept the family business thriving, and saved myself a lot of trouble restoring the manor fifty years later. I might have had children. But if all of those things had happened, you and Bob, your children and your nieces never would have existed. Elm Creek Quilts never would have been founded. And your father would not have loved your mother, in which case I know he would not be the fine man he is today."

A tear ran down Amy's face, and she ducked her head to hide it. "I don't like change," she said. "I prefer to hold on, to keep things as they are."

"You're fighting a losing battle in that case, dear," said Sylvia. She glanced around the room at the antique furniture, the years-old children's crafts decorating end tables and shelves, and suddenly she felt as if she were truly seeing Amy for the first time. It wasn't Sylvia that Amy disliked, but the unknown future. "Life is all about change, but you don't have to face the future with fear."

"I love Christmas but hate the New Year," said Amy, forcing a laugh as if she expected Sylvia to think she was a fool. "I don't like sweeping away the old year and welcoming in the new. Those moments of the past twelve months that I cherished so much are gone and they'll never come again. To me, that's a loss."

Sylvia suddenly understood why Andrew's love for her had turned Amy's world upside down. Amy thought the past was fixed, immutable, safe. Andrew's engagement to Sylvia had not only called into question her father's love for her mother, but also threatened her very way of understanding the world.

"Is something seriously wrong with me?" Amy's voice broke. "On New Year's Eve, everyone else parties and celebrates and counts down the minutes until midnight as if they can't wait to see the year end, and all the while I'm holding on to it with both fists. I'd push the ball in Times Square back up to the top of the flagpole if they'd let me."

"There's nothing wrong with you that a little perspective wouldn't cure," said Sylvia. "You aren't the only one who feels a little bit of sadness to see the old year go. After all, what's the most popular song on New Year's Eve but 'Auld Lang Syne'? Even Robert Burns felt melancholy reflecting upon days gone by, upon friends no longer near. We can't hold on to the past, it's true, but we can keep the best part of the days of 'Auld Lang Syne' in our hearts and in our memories, and we can look forward to the future with hope and resolve."

"I suppose that's all we can do," said Amy softly.

Sylvia smiled. "It's not as bad as all that. I've learned to think of the New Year as a gift. It's a blank page and you can write upon it as you wish. Sometimes we make a pledge to improve ourselves in the year ahead. My mother taught me that it's also wise to make the world a better place for someone else, even if it's only in small ways." She remembered Mrs. Compson's wise counsel. Sylvia had not taken heed in time to reconcile with her sister, but she would not make that mistake again. "A resolution is also the settlement of a dispute. Perhaps you and I and your father can make a resolution today. We're a few days shy of the New Year, but this resolution is too important to delay."

"It's not too early," said Amy. "I'm thankful that it's not too late. Besides, with three kids, I always feel like the New Year starts in September with the first day of school."

"Then let's not wait until New Year's Eve to resolve our differences." Sylvia rose and took her daughter-in-law by the hand. "Come with me. I have something to show you."

Sylvia led Amy upstairs to the guest room, where she removed the New Year's Reflections quilt from her tote bag and spread it upon the bed. "I wanted this to be a New Year's Day gift," she said, "but a day or two sooner doesn't matter. It's not quite finished, so mind the pins in the binding."

As Amy looked on, Sylvia shared the story of the New Year's Reflections quilt, from the discovery of the long-forgotten fabric stash of the Bergstrom women and the loneliness that inspired her to cut the first pieces to the unexpected path she had followed in keeping the resolution she had made that night. She described the blocks she had chosen and how each one preserved a memory of a New Year of long ago. A True Lover's Knot for Sylvia's belated acceptance of Elizabeth's marriage to Henry, and an Orange Peel for the sweetness of life she hoped they found in California. A Hatchet to mark the lead figure Claudia had found in the bowl of water by the fireside, foretelling her unhappiness in love and the severing of ties between sisters. A Wandering Foot block, a fond remembrance of her dear brother and her mother's gift for finding hope and courage in the face of uncertainty and fear. Simple patterns like those she had sewn together to make quilts for the Orphan's Home, and complex patterns to trace the tangled relationships of family united by love and chance and divided by tragedy. The Resolution Square for promises made, and Memory Chain for lessons learned. Every New Year's Eve of nostalgic farewells and each New Year's Day full of anticipation and new beginnings had been recorded in the patchwork mosaic of memories.

Sylvia would need years to tell Amy every story, every lesson she had sewn into the quilt, but for the first time since she and Andrew had announced their engagement, she believed Amy would grant her that time.

Sylvia was not the only one who shared New Year's memories from days gone by. At Sylvia's prompting, Amy recalled New Year's Eve parties in her childhood home, snowball fights and ice skating on the pond on New Year's morning, gathering around the table for a traditional meal of ham and sweet potatoes, and curling up beside her father on the sofa to watch the Rose Bowl on television. Packing up the holiday decorations on the last day of Winter Break and hauling the Christmas tree out to the curb. Settling into the New Year until it was no longer the future but the familiar present.

They lingered so long that eventually Andrew and Daniel came looking for them.

The apprehension on the men's faces when Andrew tentatively pushed open the door made both women burst out laughing. Sylvia's heart soared when Amy threw her arms around her father and murmured something in his ear. The words were meant for him alone and Sylvia would not pry, but the look of sheer happiness that lit up Andrew's face at that moment told her all would be well.

Over the next two days, Sylvia finished the New Year's Reflections quilt, often sitting in front of the fire while Amy hand-pieced a simple block nearby. As they sewed, they shared memories of New Years past, of years welcomed with excitement or with trepidation, of years that were too lovely to forget and others too sorrowful to dwell upon. Sylvia almost felt as if she were back at Elm Creek Manor, gathered together with the Bergstrom women she missed so dearly. Sylvia knew only time would allow the true bond of family to grow between her and her onetime reluctant stepdaughter, but she would resolve to be patient, to give Amy the time she needed. It was the season for hope, for joy, and for new beginnings, and Sylvia prayed she, Amy, and Andrew would be mindful of how quickly years could pass, and how unwise it was to waste a single moment in enmity.

Sylvia put the last stitch into the binding on the morning of New Year's Day, and when she presented it to Amy, it was with a heartfelt prayer that they would make the most of the fresh start the New Year offered. She knew there was no better time to reflect upon the past — mistakes and triumphs, happiness and sorrow — and look for lessons that would guide her into the future. She trusted Amy and Andrew would do the same.

Sylvia did not pretend to know what the year ahead would bring. The road before them passed through sunshine and shadow, and she could not see far beyond the first bend. But with loved ones by her side and loving memories of those who had gone before in her heart, she would move into the future with courage and hope that the best was yet to be, if she did her part to make it so.

The employees of Thorndike Press hope you have enjoyed this Large Print book. All our Thorndike and Wheeler Large Print titles are designed for easy reading, and all our books are made to last. Other Thorndike Press Large Print books are available at your library, through selected bookstores, or directly from us.

For information about titles, please call:
(800) 223-1244

or visit our Web site at:
www.gale.com/thorndike
www.gale.com/wheeler

To share your comments, please write:
Publisher
Thorndike Press
295 Kennedy Memorial Drive
Waterville, ME 04901